"You need a job, Sara," he said. "I'm offering you one. We could help each other. Please don't let me down."

The plea, and the way he said her name, startled her. In that second, she knew Jason was no domineering ogre, but simply a man desperately afraid of losing his child.

"I'll call you by tomorrow morning." She got to her feet, telling herself she had to get away, give herself a chance to calm down, to think things out.

All she'd asked for was a regular, nine-to-five, ordinary job. What she'd gotten was an offer of marriage.

Not for the normal reasons of course— Just so Jason Graham could keep his daughter.

Dear Reader,

Happy Valentine's Day! We couldn't send you flowers or chocolate hearts, but here are six wonderful new stories that capture all the magic of falling in love.

Clay Rutledge is the *Father in the Middle* in this emotional story from Phyllis Halldorson. This FABULOUS FATHER needed a new nanny for his little girl. But when he hired pretty Tamara Houston, he didn't know his adopted daughter was the child she'd once given up.

Arlene James continues her heartwarming series, THIS SIDE OF HEAVEN, with *The Rogue Who Came to Stay*. When rodeo champ Griff Shaw came home to find Joan Burton and her daughter living in his house, he couldn't turn them out. But did Joan dare share a roof with this rugged rogue?

There's mischief and romance when two sisters trade places and find love in Carolyn Zane's duet SISTER SWITCH. Meet the first half of this dazzling duo this month in *Unwilling Wife*.

In Patricia Thayer's latest book, Lafe Colter has his heart set on Michelle Royer—the one woman who wants nothing to do with him! Will *The Cowboy's Courtship* end in marriage?

Rounding out the month, Geeta Kingsley brings us *Daddy's Little Girl* and Megan McAllister finds a *Family in the Making* when she moves next door to handsome Sam Armstrong and his adorable kids in a new book by Dani Criss.

Look for more great books in the coming months from favorite authors like Diana Palmer, Elizabeth August, Suzanne Carey and many more.

Happy Reading!

Anne Canadeo
Senior Editor
Silhouette Books

Please address questions and book requests to:
Silhouette Reader Service
U.S.: 3010 Walden Ave., P.O. Box 1325, Buffalo, NY 14269
Canadian: P.O. Box 609, Fort Erie, Ont. L2A 5X3

DADDY'S
LITTLE GIRL

Geeta Kingsley

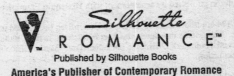

Silhouette
ROMANCE™
Published by Silhouette Books
America's Publisher of Contemporary Romance

In loving memory of my father,
Colonel R. G. Naidu,
who taught his children that
integrity has no variables

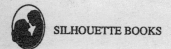 SILHOUETTE BOOKS

ISBN 0-373-19062-X

DADDY'S LITTLE GIRL

Copyright © 1995 by Geeta M. Kakade

Printed in U.S.A.

Books by Geeta Kingsley

Silhouette Romance

Faith, Hope and Love #726
Project Valentine #775
Tender Trucker #894
The Old-Fashioned Way #911
Mr. Wrong #985
Daddy's Little Girl #1062

GEETA KINGSLEY

is a former elementary school teacher who loves traveling, music, needlework and gardening. Raised in an army family, she was never lonely as long as she had books to read. She now lives in Southern California with her husband, two teenagers and the family dog. Her first published novel, *Faith, Hope and Love,* was a finalist in the Romance Writers of America's RITA competition.

Geeta believes in the triumph of the human spirit and this, along with her concern for the environment, is reflected in her characters and stories.

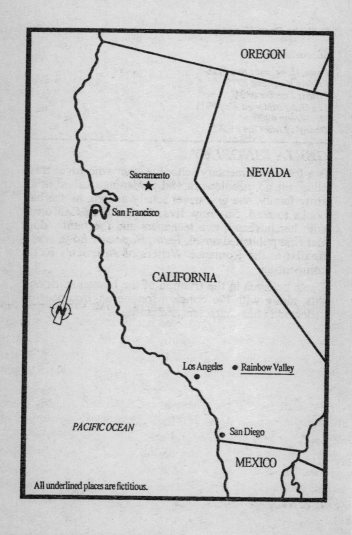

All underlined places are fictitious.

Chapter One

What kind of a man set up a job interview in a restaurant?

Sara's fingers drummed a ragged beat on the large brown envelope she'd placed on the restaurant table. The Jason Graham kind, obviously. His businesslike tones over the telephone last night had allayed her fears about the unusual venue. He'd sounded impatient and tired; as if the interview was just another chore to get over with; as if a few hours on a Friday evening was the only time he could spare.

She'd agreed to meet him at the Treasure Island, Rainbow Valley's well-known seafood restaurant. Sara stared at the fishing nets and other old shipping paraphernalia hung on the walls without really seeing them. The table Jason Graham had reserved was in a small room that held three other tables. If no one else was shown in here, they would have privacy for the interview.

A sudden shaft of worry had Sara wetting her lips. Would Jason Graham see right away that she hadn't any real job experience worth mentioning in a résumé?

She had to get this job, she just had to.

She'd lived right here in Rainbow Valley, a suburb of Los Angeles, all her life, her only real experience that of caring for a man who should have been named lifetime president of Scrooge International.

Worry undermines determination.

The book on personal motivation she had borrowed from the library had emphasized positive, not negative thinking.

I need this job.

I will get it.

It had been very kind of Claire, her best friend since high school, to slip the ad into the *Valley View* for her. Jason Graham's call was the only response she'd gotten and she had to make the most of this opportunity.

Sara closed her eyes and tried to conjure up positive pictures of the future: working in an office, taking her paycheck to the bank, living in an apartment on her own.

You'll never amount to anything. You and your mother are parasites, only capable of living off others.

Sara's eyes flew open. This was no time to let the memory of Uncle Samuel intrude. As it was, he'd had too much power for too long over her and her mother.

It was five minutes to six. Sara decided to make a quick trip to the rest room. A look at her reflection in the mirror made her wish she'd remained at the table. Nerves had driven the color from her face. The freckles on her nose stood out as if they were part of a dot-to-dot picture. All thirteen of them seemed to have popped up especially for this interview.

Sara sent a silent prayer to the patron saint of jobs.

All I want is one chance. Just one. Help me get this job.

* * *

Jason looked around the room and frowned. There was no sign of anyone in here.

"The lady must have gone to the rest room, sir," the smiling, mini-skirted hostess said. "We put you at this table."

"Thank you."

He saw the large envelope on the table right away. So, at least she was punctual. Placing the car seat that held his daughter Kelsey on the banquette seat beside him, Jason took a deep breath.

Answering the ad had not been the smartest thing he'd ever done, according to his lawyer, Moses Judah. Rowena Harris, his secretary and friend for the past eight years, had shown him the ad and pointed out it could be the answer to all his problems.

Kelsey moved in her sleep and Jason placed a hand against his daughter's flushed cheek. He would do anything for his baby girl. Anything.

They were at her table, so he . . . he must be Jason Graham. Sara's eyes widened. Her gaze sped to the seat beside him, overflowing with pink frills and lace, topped off by the face of a cherub with auburn hair.

What kind of a man brought a baby to an interview?

She forced herself to move forward.

"Mr. Graham?"

He got to his feet and looked down at her.

"Miss Adams?"

She was small and the brown suit she had on did nothing for her. Neither did the beige blouse buttoned to the top of her neck. What kind of outfit was that to wear on a first date? He'd seen nuns dressed in less.

"How are you?"

The rough palm that he'd held so briefly told him she was no stranger to hard work. Its icy coldness revealed that Sara Adams was very nervous about this meeting. Seeing her had multiplied his own fears. She wouldn't do. He shouldn't have agreed to this.

A waiter materialized as they sat down and asked what they'd like to drink. Sara ordered an iced tea and heard Jason Graham ask for a club soda.

His business suit, his tie, even the way his hair was cut, radiated power and success. Something about the width of his shoulders, the strong lines of his face, the tightness around his mouth, warned her Jason Graham wasn't a patient man. Sara's heart sank. He wouldn't hire her.

"Thank you for agreeing to meet me here."

"It was no problem." Beggars could hardly be choosers.

"Sorry I'm late, but I had to take my daughter to the doctor." Eyes, a startling chambray blue in his tanned face, hypnotized her.

"That's all right."

Jason felt his jaw tighten as the silence dragged on. Evidently the only contributions Sara Adams intended making to the conversation were these little tags on his comments. He did a quick study of her face. The large brown eyes flecked with gold that were her best feature were laced with fear. Her hair was scooped back; the color, an indeterminate shade of brown and gold.

He needed someone tough to help him, not someone who looked as if she'd lose an arm wrestling competition with a will-o'-the-wisp. His gaze fell on his daughter's face. For her sake, he had to give this meeting a try.

"Kelsey had a fever last night," he said in an effort to diffuse some of the tension. "The medicine she just had at the doctor's office has made her sleepy."

"How old is she?"

"She turned three last month."

"That's a cute age."

"Kelsey can't talk like other children her age."

The mix of pain and anger in Jason Graham's eyes warned Sara he was obviously very sensitive about it.

"I worked in a preschool," she said. "I knew a little boy who didn't say a word till he was three and a half. A specialist told his mother some children are like that."

The look he gave her told her Jason Graham didn't feel comforted. The anger in his eyes seemed to intensify.

Sara leaned back in her seat as the waiter placed their drinks and a huge basket of bread in front of them. Now what?

"Thanks, Peter. We'll be ready to order in about twenty minutes."

"Sure thing, Mr. G."

Catching the quick, scared look Sara Adams gave him as she picked up her drink, he wondered why she had placed an ad in a dating column. Sighing inwardly, he knew he had to get this over with as quickly as possible, and get Kelsey home and into bed. Sara Adams had made an effort to come here, though, so the least he could do was talk to her and buy her dinner.

"You said on the telephone you haven't worked for a while because you've been taking care of your uncle?"

"Yes. He died four weeks ago."

"What was wrong with him?"

"He had a stroke three years ago that left him partially paralyzed, and another one ten months ago that left him bedridden."

That caught his interest. Nursing an invalid took patience and loyalty. If Sara Adams really possessed those two qualities, his search had ended. What did it matter what she looked like? "Your ad also mentioned you don't mind traveling?"

"No. I—I mean yes. I—I mean..." The brow he lifted made Sara stop and swallow hard before she said, "I don't mind traveling."

Jason Graham studied the fishing nets on the walls as if he'd run out of questions for the time being. One look at his face told Sara she'd scored zero so far.

You've got to learn to sell yourself, kid, Claire had said after Sara had returned from the last unsuccessful interview. *Self-promotion's the name of the game.*

Failure loomed so close on the horizon she could almost reach out and touch it. Desperation had her clearing her throat and saying, "I'm very reliable and hardworking. You won't be disappointed, if you give me a chance."

Jason didn't miss the rasp in her voice. Was she that desperate to get married that she had to resort to pleading?

"I'm a self-starter, honest and punctual."

The anxious eyes that shied away from his made him stop and think. The woman across from him might be just what he was looking for, after all. For the past few weeks, since he'd realized a business marriage might be the answer to his problems, Jason had considered the women he knew. Most of the women in his circle reminded him of Diana. He had no time for a demanding, spoiled wife, and he definitely didn't want any emotional entanglements of any kind this time around.

It was very important that he remain the one in control of this strange situation from beginning to end. He looked at Kelsey again and his misgivings were shoved aside. His daughter came first. A pang of guilt shot through him at the thought that he might be taking advantage of Sara Adams. For a moment the ridiculous idea that she was almost as vulnerable as Kelsey crossed his mind, but then he dismissed it. Though he had no other choice, he would make sure Ms. Adams got a good deal.

Kelsey moved in her sleep, and Jason patted her till she'd settled down again. A hand against her cheek told him her fever had receded.

"Is your passport in order?" he asked.

Sara's breath caught in her throat. Was he offering her the job, after all? "Yes. I took a cruise to Europe with my uncle a year ago."

Jason nodded. "Though this trip's only going to last six weeks, I live in England five months out of the year. Will that bother you?"

"No." Her heartbeat quickened and hope made her sit up straighter. A job on the moon wouldn't bother her.

"I use London as a base for my business in Europe. Now a new market is opening up, which I'm interested in cornering."

"What business are you in?" she asked quickly, careful to keep her voice neutral. It was the first time he'd mentioned actual work. Maybe Jason Graham just took a long time getting to the point.

"I've developed a variation of the new electronic braking system being used in cars. My company's in the fledgling stages. To keep the overheads low, I do most of the marketing myself."

Sara listened eagerly. She knew very little about electronic brakes, but she was willing to learn.

"Do you really like children?"

Sara frowned slightly. It was an odd digression, but she supposed from the frequent glances he threw his daughter, that Kelsey was on his mind.

"Yes."

Their gazes met and Sara looked away quickly. There was something unnerving about Jason Graham's stare. It was as if his gaze penetrated below the surface, probing the secret places in her mind.

"I always take Kelsey with me when I travel." He reached for a roll, and buttered it generously.

Some of the mystery began to clear as Sara pieced their fragmented conversation together. Jason Graham wanted someone to take care of Kelsey. It was a far cry from the office job she wanted, but it had advantages she couldn't overlook. Assuming Jason Graham wanted live-in help even when he wasn't traveling, she wouldn't have to worry about the problem and expense of an apartment or food. And if she was careful with the money she made, she'd be that much closer to the freedom she dreamed of by the end of this job.

The reminder that beggars couldn't be choosers made Sara figure it was time to get down to the specifics of this job. "You want me to watch Kelsey?"

Jason Graham frowned. "I suppose there will be times when you might have to, but that's only part of it."

"Only part of it?" Sara looked at the handsome man across from her and caught herself before frowning. What *did* he want?

"I need more than a baby-sitter. Kelsey's mother—my wife, Diana—died six months ago. Now Diana's mother has suddenly decided she wants custody of Kelsey. I love my daughter more than anything in the world, Ms. Adams. To keep her, I have to prove I can provide a stable home background for her."

Sara nodded, her uncertainty vanishing. She was as stable as Mount Everest. There was something she had to say, though.

"I need to have some time to myself."

Jason watched her carefully. That was fine with him, but he'd better make it clear this was not going to be the kind of marriage she envisioned. "You'll have plenty of time to yourself," he assured her. "You'll have your own bedroom, and as much freedom as you want."

Sara frowned. Wait a minute. She'd taken it for granted she wouldn't be sharing a room with Kelsey, and caring for a three-year-old would hardly give her a great deal of free time—

"To get back to what I was saying," Jason Graham interrupted her thoughts, "The pediatric specialist says there's nothing wrong with Kelsey that time won't cure, but Dee-dee is trying to prove it's my traveling life-style that's interfering with Kelsey's progress."

Sara's stomach automatically contracted at the anger in Jason Graham's voice, then relaxed. This was a different kind of anger from Uncle Samuel's uncontrollable fits of temper. Jason Graham's anger was directed inward, not at her. The tense mouth, the muscle that ticked so clearly in his jaw, told Sara that deep down Jason Graham blamed himself for his daughter's condition. Responding to his pain came as naturally as breathing.

"Kelsey will talk when she's ready," she said reassuringly.

"I hope so. There's nothing wrong with Kelsey's hearing, so I just have to be patient."

Jason Graham reached over and ran his knuckles down the side of his daughter's chubby face. His expression as he looked at his child was filled with love.

Sara's heart melted. Jason Graham had suffered an enormous loss when his wife died. It wasn't fair that he should lose the child he obviously loved so much. She needed this job and by taking it, she would be helping little Kelsey and her father. How could she say no?

Unable to miss the softening in her eyes, Jason knew he'd succeeded, somehow, in gaining her interest. Good. Moses had warned him that he would have to be very clear about the terms of the prenuptial agreement, though. He couldn't run the risk of being taken to the cleaners later. As he looked at the woman seated opposite him, Jason felt like smiling for the first time that evening. He was positive the very thought of blackmailing someone would terrify Sara Adams.

"Could you be ready to leave for England in about ten days?"

"Are you offering me the job?" With effort, Sara kept her excitement out of her voice. She needed to hear him say the words.

Jason nodded, surprised by the flare of relief in her eyes. That was an odd way to refer to marriage. He didn't want her making any false assumptions, so he said quickly, "I know this is a very unusual approach, Sara, but for me it's the only way out of a difficult situation."

"I understand. I'll do all I can to help," Sara replied earnestly. A celestial chorus seemed to be singing in her head. *She had the job.*

"Is there someone you want me to meet, or talk to? Your family? Your parents?"

The celestial chorus stopped abruptly. Looking quietly at him, Sara blinked. That was a strange question. As an adult, she didn't need to ask anyone's permission before she took a job.

"I don't have anyone."

The words renewed Jason's uneasiness. No matter how much he paid her, it didn't hide the fact that he was, in effect, using Sara Adams. But what other choices did he have? He had to make sure his bases were covered where the lawsuit was concerned. He also had to be in England in two weeks to negotiate a million-dollar contract that was in the works. Postponement, even for a few months, meant he'd lose the deal. Discoveries in the electronic world were being made every day. If he waited, a dozen other people would come up with the same idea he had. Manufacturers in Third World countries would offer the product three times cheaper than he could. Being first and being fast made the difference between success and failure. He *had* to get this settled and return to England soon.

"My secretary mailed you some references," he told Sara Adams. "Did you get them?"

Why on earth would *he* mail her references? "Not yet. I didn't check the mailbox before I left the house today. I've brought my résumé with me." Sara slid the brown envelope across the table.

Jason's eyes narrowed. Why would someone bring a résumé to a first date? *He* was providing references because he wanted Sara Adams to know she could trust him. "I brought Kelsey with me, so you could meet her right away. As I said before, she's the most important person in my life."

"I can see that. I'll take good care of her." Impatience began threading its way through her. Wasn't he at least going to take a look at her résumé?

"Loyalty and commitment are very important to me," Jason said seriously, looking straight into her eyes. He couldn't afford to make any mistakes. "Do you have any personal entanglements that would get in the way of our arrangement?"

"Personal entanglements?" What was he talking about?

"A boyfriend? A lover?" Moses had told him to make sure there was no one who might instigate Sara Adams to cause trouble later.

Her face went bright red as she answered. "No."

He hated intruding in her personal life, but it had to be done.

"It's absolutely imperative you realize that though this is an unusual job, I will not permit any kind of familiarity. As far as you and I are concerned, you are my employee, nothing more, nothing less."

"Of course." Sara couldn't prevent the stuffiness that crept into her voice. She wasn't the type to straighten her employer's tie or climb into his lap to discuss his daughter's progress.

Jason heard the note of hauteur. He'd offended her, but it couldn't be helped. "There will be times when we're both in awkward situations, but handled professionally, I think we can make this work."

"I do, too." Did the man consider diaper changing and cleaning up after a kid "awkward situations"?

"I know tomorrow is Saturday, but as I'm rushed for time, would you mind meeting me at the lawyer's office at ten?"

Sara's brows shot up. She seemed to have lost the thread of Jason Graham's conversation again. "Lawyer's office?"

"We have to go over the terms of the prenuptial agreement before we can get a special license."

Sara stared at Jason Graham. Had nervousness affected her auditory system? Maybe she should have borrowed Uncle Samuel's hearing aid for the occasion.

"P-prenuptial agreement?" she stammered finally.

Jason nodded. Why on earth was she looking so surprised? Surely she couldn't be that naive. "It's very common these days, and it's the best way of protecting the interests of both parties before marriage."

"M-marriage?"

Jason nodded again, confused. Sara Adams had gone white. "Surely," he said impatiently, "you had marriage in mind when you put that ad into the Catch Basin?"

"The Catch Basin?" That was the Personals section. She never even read the matrimonial page of the *Valley View*. She only knew about the section because Claire always talked about the ads she put in there for herself.

Jason bent and picked up the magazine from the side pocket of Kelsey's diaper bag. It was opened at the page her ad was on.

"My secretary knows how concerned I am about the lawsuit. She showed me the ad and suggested a business marriage might provide the perfect solution to my problem."

Sara stared at the highlighted blurb blankly before her gaze went to the top of the page. Horror jumped in to share the space with surprise. That was *not* her ad. Not only had Claire changed the wording, she'd put it on the *matrimonial* page of the *Valley View*. How could she have done something like that?

Cleaning the house and packing Uncle Samuel's clothes and a collection of thirty-five years of things he'd never thrown away had kept Sara so busy she hadn't thought to check the ad herself.

"It's all a mistake."

Jason's eyes narrowed. Why the sudden about-face?

"There's no mistake," he said grimly. "You put in an ad. I answered it."

"My friend was supposed to put this ad into the Jobs Wanted column. I don't know how it got into the Catch Basin section." Face red with embarrassment and her heart sinking, Sara cursed inwardly. She should never have agreed to Claire's plan in the first place.

"You see, I needed a job badly," she explained quickly. "My friend Claire works for the *Valley View*. She said no one would notice if she slipped an extra ad in...." Sara trailed off, staring at the tablecloth. Her mouth was running away with her. She shouldn't have told him what Claire had done.

Making quick decisions was part of being a businessman. Jason realized what was going on. Sara hadn't been looking for a husband. Which meant, unless he did something—and fast—that he would lose her. Metaphoric arm twisting was something he'd never indulged in, but in this instance it was the only thing he could think of.

"I answered the ad in good faith," he said sternly, suppressing the rising tide of guilt. "Even if it was a mix-up, what do you have to lose? You need a job, I'm offering you one."

"I can't marry you," Sara said miserably.

"If you won't consider my offer, I'll have to call the *Valley View* and complain about what's happened. I just don't have the time to look for someone else now, and I'm sure as hell not going to let Kelsey suffer because you're getting cold feet."

"It's all a mistake," Sara said, swallowing hard. Her heart beat so loudly, she could barely hear herself speak. "You *can't* complain to the *Valley View*. Claire will lose her job. She has a little boy to support, and her husband refuses to pay alimony."

"Try me," Jason said grimly. He had problems, too, and the fear that he would lose Kelsey overcame everything else.

"I—I need some time to think." Sara put a hand up and rubbed her forehead as if to get rid of the warring pictures there. He obviously wanted her to take on the job of his wife so that he could win the custody suit. But how could she possibly—

"I can give you till tomorrow morning."

Jason Graham's face didn't show an inch of give. Her first impression of him being stern and tough had been right, after all. Their gazes clashed, and Sara felt as if she were drowning in the power of his will.

"You need a job, Sara. I'm offering you one. We could help each other. Please don't let me down."

The plea, and the way he said her name, startled her. In that second she knew Jason Graham was no domineering ogre; simply a man desperately afraid of losing his child.

"I'll call you by tomorrow morning." She got to her feet and held her hand out.

"What about dinner?"

"I can't eat anything now. Thanks for the drink."

She turned, telling herself she had to get away, give herself a chance to calm down, to think things out. Leaving the restaurant and getting into Uncle Samuel's old car, she rested her head on the wheel.

Who was it up there, anyway, who was in charge of jobs? All she'd asked for was a regular nine-to-five. An ordinary job. What she'd gotten was enough to shake any human being's faith in patron saints and prayer. She'd been offered marriage.

Not for the normal reasons, of course. Just so Jason Graham could keep his daughter.

Sara's vision blurred as she backed out of the parking lot. On top of it all was Claire. She'd only been trying to help. She couldn't let Claire suffer.

What had made Jason Graham decide she was the right candidate for the job? Did she have a stamp on her forehead that said Easily Bullied. Plenty Of Experience Slaving For A Manipulative Man?

She couldn't possibly do this, she argued to herself as she drove. Marriage to Jason Graham would only be a replay of her life so far. Sara could never enter any kind of bondage willingly again. Not if she starved.

It's a business arrangement.

She'd dreamed about marriage; about finding someone who would love her; someone with whom she could share the rest of her life. Her dreams held a house, a warm, loving man, children. *What kind of a man suggested marriage could be a business arrangement?*

Pulling into the driveway of Uncle Samuel's house, Sara stared at it. The four-bedroom house with an indoor swimming pool on an acre of land was as close to a prison as she ever wanted to be.

The mailbox at the end of the drive held two envelopes. One was from Jason Graham's office, the other was from Uncle Samuel's lawyer. Her fingers shook as she ripped open the latter. If only she could have a little more time to find another job.

Your uncle specifically mentioned in his will that your occupancy of the house was to be terminated a month following his death. It was not to be extended under any circumstances.

I regret . . .

The rest of the words ran together as angry tears filled Sara's eyes. Even from his grave, Uncle Samuel had the power to hurt. Her mother had worked herself to death for him and he hadn't cared. Sara herself had given him twenty-four years of her life. That was twenty-four years too many. She had to get out of here as soon as possible.

An hour later, after a shower and a sandwich, Sara paced the kitchen floor. Claire had taken Bobby to her mother's in Sacramento for the weekend, so she couldn't even call her. How could Claire have messed up so badly?

It wasn't any use worrying about that now. She had to reach some sort of a decision soon. The facts were simple.

Sara needed a job and a place to stay. Jason Graham needed a wife.

The ramifications overwhelmed her. Marriage wasn't a state one entered into lightly. Despite being plain and unattractive, she wasn't willing to give up on her dreams.

Agreeing to Jason Graham's ridiculous proposition would mean giving up her new independence. She didn't want permanent ties to anyone right now, even if Jason Graham did think of those ties as business ones.

By threatening to complain about Claire, Jason Graham had proven he was just like her uncle. He didn't understand honest mistakes. He was only aware of his own needs. All man. All self-involved.

The next instant, honesty demanded she amend that conclusion. The tender way he'd looked at his daughter popped into her mind. She couldn't fault his motivation. He loved his child and he wanted to keep her. He was simply doing what he thought would ensure that result. A parent had those inalienable rights.

She reached for the second envelope that had been in her mailbox, Claire's voice ringing in her ears.

You've got to stop thinking about others and start learning to put yourself first, before it's too late.

That was Sara's first challenge.

Chapter Two

Jason Graham had enclosed letters of reference from a bank president, a minister, two lawyers and a woman who had worked for him for eight years. The words "good character," "absolute integrity" and "a man of principles," were repeated over and over again. The woman, Rowena Harris, had added that Jason Graham was a wonderful employer and father. Since his wife's death, he'd often worked through the night to make time for his daughter.

Sara walked over to the kitchen window. The mountains in the background, their peaks reflecting the glow of the setting sun, offered no solutions. *Smart people create their own opportunities,* the calendar on the kitchen wall said. Sara looked at it, and her eyes narrowed. Maybe there was something she could do with this situation.

She had to think of Jason Graham's offer as a door to the freedom she wanted. Helping him win the lawsuit shouldn't take more than six months, max. The amount he'd mentioned he was willing to pay was very generous. Quick calculations in her head told her she'd have more than enough money to pay a year's rent on an apartment by then.

But marriage... Sara's heart still refused to agree to a marriage that was a business arrangement. That was one dream she wasn't willing to give up on. Dare she voice the only alternative she could come up with to Jason Graham? She could try. Resolution shot up her spine and flooded her brain, clearing fear away. Helping Jason Graham keep his daughter was one thing. Allowing him to bully her into marriage was another.

Sara was plain, not stupid. Living with Uncle Samuel had taught her that men took what they wanted, riding rough-shod over feelings in the process. There were too many bitter examples around for her to ever forget that. The sadness that had always clouded her mother's eyes. Claire's bitter divorce. And if Sara's father had been as great as her mother had said he was, why hadn't he waited around *after* they'd made a baby?

She'd learned that there was only one person who could stand up for Sara Adams. It was a job she had to do herself.

Sara stopped pacing and reached for the phone. She had to get this over with before her courage deserted her.

"I'll take the job, if you'll consider my proposal," she said as soon as Jason Graham answered the telephone.

"What proposal is that?"

Sara didn't let the crispness in Jason Graham's voice deter her.

"I'll travel with you as your fiancée, not your wife."

"How will that help me in court?"

"An engagement can be just as effective as a marriage. A good lawyer can convince the court you are in the *process* of setting up a stable home for Kelsey. I think the fact we've become engaged, so that all three of us can adjust to a new situation before we get married, will make sense to a judge. Besides, you can also say you wanted to give me time to be sure about my feelings, that you want this relationship to last forever. Patience will make more sense in a courtroom than the fact you've jumped into marriage with a complete stranger.''

The determination in Sara's voice was at odds with the way her fingers twisted the telephone cord.

''What do you have against marriage?'' Jason demanded.

She took a deep breath. ''Marriage is not a state one enters and exits lightly. Not in my book, at least.''

''I'll have to give it some thought,'' Jason said reluctantly. ''Dee-dee might bring up something to the effect our living in sin is having a bad influence on Kelsey.''

Sara felt herself go bright red at the thought people would think they were lovers. ''She'd have to prove it first, wouldn't she? Isn't she aware that some people still get engaged in this day and age, without living together in the sense you mean?''

There was a pause and then Jason Graham said, ''It might just work. I'll check with my lawyer and call you back.''

Sara thanked him and said goodbye. Hanging up, she realized she'd risked everything on that one call. Standing by what mattered most meant she might fall by her ideals and lose the only real job offer she was likely to have.

Jason poured himself a cup of black coffee. He had to catch up with the work he'd brought home from the office. Kelsey had woken up, had some chicken noodle soup and gone back to sleep.

Jason looked at the dark liquid in the mug, wondering about Sara Adams. He had to agree with one part of what she'd said. No one, not even Dee-dee Smythe, would be able to picture someone as straight arrow as Sara Adams living in sin.

Something in her eyes had told him she wasn't putting on an act. The fact she wasn't too scared to argue with him now proved she wasn't as malleable as he'd imagined. Under the quiet, unassuming exterior, Sara Adams was stronger than he'd thought.

He felt strangely keyed up as he thought of the courage she came wrapped in. He hadn't asked what her circumstances were, but he knew she needed a job desperately. His brows drew together. Not so desperately that she would fall in with anything he wanted, though. What did she have against marriage?

Marriage is not a state one enters and exits lightly. Not in my book . . .

He hadn't missed the catch in her voice. Did Sara Adams have dreams of marriage being a state of happily-ever-after? When she'd said that, he'd opened his mouth to say something, then closed it. The fact that he'd had a rough ride on the marriage roller coaster didn't give him the right to stomp on anyone else's dreams.

Jason felt his jaw clench. Had he been wrong about Sara Adams? They hadn't even finalized things, and she was dictating terms to him. Women always took a mile even before you'd given them an inch.

As his wife, she would have everything she needed. Money, the best clothes, a luxurious life-style. According to the terms of the agreement Moses had drawn up, whoever helped Jason would receive a large bonus on termination of the agreement, as well.

Moses had reluctantly agreed marriage would provide Jason with infallible evidence that he was trying to set up a stable home for Kelsey. The lawyer, who'd known him since

Jason's pre-Diana days, had pointed out very quickly that answering an ad, however, was risky. Extremely risky. Only opportunists chose that route. Jason had to be very careful that he wasn't taken in by someone sharper than himself.

Jason knew all about clever, selfish women. Diana had taught him an unforgettable lesson in that department. No one was going to take him for an emotional ride twice. He was done with love and all that sort of thing.

Rowena had persuaded him that there was nothing wrong with answering the ad, considering his circumstances. Her niece had met a nice man through the same paper. A smart woman would seize the opportunity of making some good money for doing very little in return.

The idea had been a rope thrown to a drowning man. Marriage seemed like the only way to make sure Kelsey stayed with him.

A willing woman and a legal arrangement had sounded like the only way to have it all.

Sara Adams wasn't willing, though.

The realization shook him because he believed one could buy anything if one was willing to pay the price. Ms. Adams was different. In spite of her desperate need of a job, she had risked losing everything by standing up for whatever it was she believed in. That set her apart from the women he knew.

Twin prongs of worry and guilt gripped him in a vise. For an instant he wanted to tell her it had all been a mistake and they should just forget the whole thing. A glance at Kelsey's innocent, sleeping face, however, and Jason felt the familiar fierce protectiveness surge through his body. No one was going to take his baby daughter away from him. Circumstances had him backed into a corner. He had no other choice except to give Sara Adams's way a try.

Hiring her also had an added benefit. Sara Adams wasn't the kind of woman he was attracted to, normally, which would prevent the complications Moses had warned him about. As for the odd protectiveness she inspired...he shrugged dismissively. It was only because she looked so young.

If he had an employee evaluation sheet in front of him, Jason would have Sara Adams down as quiet, undemanding, passive. A follower, not a leader. Except for that unexpected streak of stubbornness, he'd judged her correctly.

He picked up his coffee and sipped it. As it trickled down his throat, he told himself he was right on one score. Sara Adams would be no trouble. No trouble at all.

The ringing of the doorbell startled Sara. It echoed through the empty house. Had Uncle Samuel's lawyer come by to pick up the key in person to make sure she'd left everything in good condition?

Sara's heart lurched when she opened the door. "Mr. Graham?"

What on earth was he doing here so early on a Sunday morning?

"It's Jason, Sara."

She flushed. He'd told her that twice yesterday in the lawyer's office, as well. "I'm sorry."

He looked bigger than ever in charcoal gray sweats that were a perfect foil for his dark hair and blue eyes. For the first time she noticed the tiredness that shadowed his face.

"Is something wrong?"

Maybe he'd had second thoughts about the whole thing and had come to tell her so. Sara's heart sank. She'd have to move into the dormitory at the Y till she found another job.

"Nothing's wrong. May I come in?"

"Of course." She stood aside, feeling awkward. She'd been feeling awkward, and a bit dizzy ever since he'd called her back to agree to her proposal.

"I thought I'd help you move." She caught the faint whiff of his soap, a lemony cologne, and the scent of baby powder as he passed her.

"Move?" Sara asked blankly.

"Yes. Yesterday you said you would come over early this morning by cab. I thought I'd help you instead," Jason said innocently. The truth was, as much as he'd wanted to help, he'd also wanted to see the house she'd lived in, know a little more about the enigma that was Sara Adams. Yesterday, when they'd met at Moses' office, she'd worn the brown suit again and Moses had looked very uneasy. They'd gone over the terms of the contract and Moses had asked her if she'd like to have her own lawyer go over it. Sara had looked surprised and told him she didn't have a lawyer and she trusted him.

Moses had gone beet red. Jason would never forget the look on the lawyer's face as Sara had said, "There is just one thing, though. Mr. Graham's paying me a very generous salary. There's no need for this bonus you mention in the contract."

Moses had turned strange after that. While Sara had sat in the waiting room, Moses had told Jason sternly that people like Sara Adams were rare. In all his forty years of practicing law, he'd never met anyone who'd turned money down. He'd looked worried as he'd said she was a nice young lady, and he hoped they were doing the right thing. Reluctantly he'd handed Jason the report one of his investigators had prepared on Sara. Jason hadn't liked the fact that Moses had had Sara investigated, but his lawyer had pointed out it was good common sense to do so, these days.

Because Kelsey was involved, Jason had forced himself to read the report.

There had been very little in it that Jason didn't know already. She'd lived all her life with her mother and uncle in Rainbow Valley. Her mother had died five and a half years ago, her uncle a month ago. Sara Adams had worked part-time in a preschool for almost five years. She had no boyfriend.

It had sounded like a pretty lonely existence.

Now as Jason glanced around at the cardboard cartons in the hall he realized there were about twenty of them and they were huge. He frowned. "We could take the smallest of these and then have someone get the rest."

Sara Adams gave him a puzzled look and then followed his glance to the cartons. "These aren't mine," she said quickly.

"Whose are they?"

"My uncle's. His lawyer asked me to pack his things."

More boxes through a wooden arch caught Jason's eyes. He moved toward an elaborate dining room. Six huge boxes covered most of the marble floor.

"You did all this?"

His eyes went from the Aubusson rug on the floor to the collector's painting on the wall. Why hadn't packers been hired?

"Only the small things. Movers are going to get the expensive stuff."

"Do you have any staff to help you?"

"There was only Uncle and me here."

"You shouldn't have had to pack these things, Sara." He caught one of her hands and turned it over. There was a two-inch-long, open scratch on the back of it.

Sara snatched her hand back and hid it behind her. It tingled where he'd touched it. "It's all right. I didn't mind."

"Do you have a bandage?"

She wet her lips. "My bag's in the kitchen."

He followed her there, taking note of more boxes. A slow burn of anger was building within him. Was her uncle's lawyer taking advantage of her?

He watched her rummage through her handbag. Taking out a bandage, she tore it open.

"Here, let me." He took the plaster strip from her and placed it over the cut. "That's better."

"Th-thank you." She looked up at him, and Jason was reminded of a bird he'd found when he was about ten. It had been injured in a storm and it had trembled just the way Sara Adams was now. He looked into her eyes. Something stirred within him. She was a golden brown owl; one that, for some reason, was scared of him.

"Would you like some coffee?"

He let her hand go and stepped away. What was wrong with him? "That wouldn't be a bad idea." Moving to the window, he stared at the mountains outside. "You have a beautiful view."

"When Uncle Samuel bought the land thirty-five years ago, there were very few houses out here. He got a real bargain. Would you like to go and see the view from upstairs, while I get the coffee?"

Jason nodded. "I'll do that."

His tour of the house was quick. He didn't waste much time on the view—he was too busy counting boxes. Sixty. Sara Adams had packed sixty boxes in all. The slow burn of anger inside was turning into a blaze.

He stood in the room that must be hers because it had an overnight bag on the bed. Jason frowned. It was the smallest room on the floor, and the plainest one in the whole house.

A cotton rug on the floor, plain white curtains at the windows, a cheap bedspread on the single bed. The other rooms had furniture he'd have liked to own. This one had a chest of drawers that looked as if it was a garage sale reject.

"I need to get a few things upstairs. I won't be long," Sara said as he returned to the kitchen. "I'm sorry I had to use a disposable cup for your coffee, but everything else has been packed."

"That's fine."

Watching her leave, Jason frowned. Yesterday Sara had mentioned the house had been left to an organization. Why had Sara's uncle left the house to charity? She'd lived here all her life. Why wasn't the house hers now? As for the lawyer... Jason's eyes narrowed. He'd get the man's name and have Moses talk to the guy.

The phone rang three times before Jason picked it up. "Hello?"

"Is Sara Adams there?"

Jason didn't like the tone of the man's voice at the other end. "May I ask who's calling?"

"This is Sid Greer from the law firm of Greer and Hancock. I'm calling to see if everything's packed and cleaned."

That explained the folded draperies he'd seen on the beds upstairs and the marks of a steam cleaner on the carpet.

"I'd also like to know if the garden's been mowed. There's a party interested in seeing the place today and I was wondering if Sara could stay on and show the house?"

Jason's brows snapped together. He'd seen the extent of the yard from the upstairs windows. At least three-quarters of an acre was grass. That wasn't a garden out there...it was a damned park.

"You'll have to hire new help," he barked into the phone. "My fiancée is leaving with me now. Any further communications will have to be made through my lawyer, Moses

Judah. I also expect you to compensate my fiancée for the hours she has put in cleaning this place and packing up in the last few days."

"Now, look here . . ." the voice at the other end blustered. "I don't know who you are, but you have no right to be there. I'm—"

Jason had had enough. "The name's Jason Graham. CEO and owner of Graham Electronics. I have every right to be here and help my fiancée move out. Locking the front door is the last thing she's going to do for you. My lawyer will be in touch with you about that money you owe her."

Sara stood frozen in the doorway. Why was Jason Graham defending her?

"Is that Sid?" she asked as he hung up. "I'll just call him and see what he wants."

Jason caught her hand as it reached for the telephone. "No," he said. "You're not doing one thing more here. You heard what I told that guy. He's been using you. Let's go."

Sara bit her lip. Jason Graham didn't understand. She'd done all this because it canceled the last of her debt to Uncle Samuel, not because she'd had to. Even she knew Sid had been taking advantage of her.

"Sara?"

She picked up her handbag from the counter and turned away. She could always call Sid later. Right now Jason sounded annoyed, and she didn't want to start their working relationship off on the wrong foot.

He picked up the overnight bag she'd placed by the door. "Where's the rest of your stuff?"

"I've got it."

Sara picked up the old cardboard carton near the front door, wishing it wasn't tied with string, wishing she had luggage worth calling that.

She saw the flare in Jason Graham's eyes and said quickly, "All the suitcases belong to Uncle Samuel."

And she hadn't felt like taking even one after all she'd done here? She could have at least picked a good, strong box instead of the one she held in her arms. His first thought, that it was all an act to impress him, didn't last two seconds. Sara Adams hadn't known he was coming. So angry he couldn't trust himself to speak, Jason turned and marched to the front door.

Had he made a mistake after all? Subduing the protective surge threatening to overwhelm him, Jason focused on what was important. Sara Adams wasn't going to be much use to him if she couldn't stand up for herself. Dee-dee had claws that were sharpened every day on the metal post of her brain . . . they'd rip the little golden brown owl to shreds.

An hour later Sara looked around the bedroom Mrs. Garcia, Jason's housekeeper, had shown her to.

"Mr. Graham said he wants you in the bedroom next to his," the housekeeper had said with a smile.

Sara felt herself flush. As his fiancée, that was probably something quite normal. He'd mentioned his mother-in-law visited often. They'd have to do this right.

For a moment she thought of his anger earlier and fear that she'd fail him overwhelmed her. He'd driven her here in silence, deposited her box and her overnight bag in the foyer, called for Mrs. Garcia, and then disappeared with a curt "I'll see you later."

One day at a time.

The worst jobs were best tackled that way. Sara looked out her window, trying to take her mind off her fear. Jason Graham's house was set on a hilltop and had a wonderful view of both the mountains and the tiny cities at their foothills. Part of a master-planned community a developer had created in Rainbow Valley, everything about this wonderful, modern house was different from the one she'd been raised in.

Her bedroom had two bookshelves, a table and a chair, and a dresser. The walk-in closet was big enough to hold the room she'd slept in at Uncle Samuel's.

She would take wall-to-wall carpeting and light, modern furniture over wooden floors that needed constant polishing and heavy antique furniture that was a pain to dust and keep clean any day.

A quick look around showed she'd put everything away neatly. Picking up the cardboard box she'd packed her things in, Sara decided to take it downstairs and ask Mrs. Garcia where she could dispose of it. The housekeeper had mentioned something about Jason taking Kelsey to a friend's house for a visit. Maybe she could help the housekeeper with something till they came back.

Jason shifted a sleeping Kelsey on his shoulder, stopping dead in the kitchen doorway. Rowena had invited them for lunch and Kelsey was tuckered out after playing with the new Irish setter mix puppy Rowena had just picked up from the humane shelter. He wanted a soda, but he couldn't get into the kitchen.

There was a bottom making its way backward toward the door. It was too small to belong to Mrs. Garcia, and he'd seen that faded skirt a few hours ago. He was staring at Sara's bottom.

His eyes narrowed as her movements told him what she was doing. She was washing his kitchen floor, humming under her breath. Grimly he carried Kelsey up to her room and put her into her bed, making sure the guard rail was secure and the baby monitor was switched on before going back downstairs.

Sara had just reached the doorway. She got to her feet, still humming, and stood looking at the kitchen floor.

"It does look nice," she said to herself.

He couldn't understand what there was to admire in a kitchen floor. "Do you mind telling me what you're doing?"

She spun around, her mouth opening in a perfect O. "I—I'm cleaning the kitchen floor."

The memory of that spotlessly clean house he had picked her up from came to mind. Maybe she was one of those women who had to have something to clean.

"We have a mop, you know," he began conversationally.

"On your hands and knees is the only way to get a floor cleaned properly," she said.

"Not for my fiancée, it isn't." A slow anger was creeping its way through him. Jason didn't want to think of how rough her palm felt, or how many years she might have cleaned floors. Taking the rag from her hand, he dropped it into the sink. "Cleaning is Mrs. Garcia's job." He turned to the housekeeper, who had appeared in the doorway. "Isn't it?"

"*Sí,*" said Mrs. Garcia nervously.

"She didn't ask me to help." Sara was quick in her defense of the housekeeper. "I just wanted something to do."

Jason took one of Sara's wrists. "Come with me, Sara. We need to talk."

He steered her in the direction of the garden. The landscaper had placed a wrought-iron bench under a jacaranda in the front yard. Reaching it, Jason gestured "Sit."

She sat, moving as far into the corner as she could get. "I'm sorry."

Jason ran a hand over his face. Personally he didn't care what she did. If cleaning floors was her thing, he'd have the carpeting removed and let her have the run of the place. But he had to match his wits against Dee-dee's.

"Sara, let me tell you something about Kelsey's grandmother. Dee-dee is sharp. If she had seen you doing that floor, she would have known right away that there was something very wrong about this engagement."

Sara studied him seriously, then said, "You mean, you wouldn't get engaged to a woman who did housework?"

"Exactly."

"What kind of a woman would you get engaged to in the normal course of things, Mr.—I mean, Jason?"

He stared at her face, noticing how her exertions had left her all pink and flushed. Resisting the urge to touch her soft cheek, he answered her question. "Someone smart and modern. An extrovert. Someone able to hold her own against Dee-dee. Someone fun to be with."

She'd scored zero again. Sara was beginning to understand why Jason had answered her ad. Claire had substituted words like "upbeat" for her original "diligent," "attractive" for "conscientious."

"I'll try to be the way you want," Sara said on a subdued note. "Claire changed the wording of the ad. I'm really not upbeat, or attractive, you know."

Jason sighed. He knew. Upbeat was out of the question, Sara was far too serious for that, but attractive wasn't. The golden brown eyes fixed on him. Transparent with honesty and earnestness, they were the most beautiful he had ever seen.

"If you'd like to get someone else . . ."

"No." He was surprised by how quickly the word came out. "No. We just have to get used to each other, that's all. Now, if you'll excuse me, I have some work to do."

Sara watched him walk away, choosing not to investigate the relief flooding through her. Leaving would not have been easy, and it wouldn't have been just because of the money. Shaking her head bemusedly, she focused her thoughts. She had a second challenge to tackle before she met the first. She had to make sure she didn't let Jason Graham down. Leaning back in the seat, she gave some thought to the matter of being his fiancée.

Jason stood in the marble entryway of his house and listened. Kelsey's loud chuckles indicated his daughter was in the family room. The sound of her happiness brought a smile to his face, easing his tiredness. It was only Tuesday and Sara had barely been here forty-eight hours and already he knew he'd never heard the sound of Kelsey's laughter so frequently. That alone justified the bargain he'd made with Sara. She and Kelsey had taken to each other from the word go.

He ran upstairs, yanking at his tie. Shedding his suit quickly, he pulled on old jeans and a sweatshirt and headed downstairs, eager to see Kelsey. Opening the door to the family room, he realized Sara and his daughter were too immersed in their game to notice him. Kelsey was hiding behind the couch, while Sara, on all fours, was pretending to look for her. Her bottom wiggled high in the air as she pretended to search behind a recliner.

She picked up cushions and looked under the coffee table as she said, "Where is Kelsey hiding? I just can't find her."

Judging from his daughter's giggles, she loved the game. Suddenly Kelsey looked up and saw him, and the next minute she ran to him. Aware Sara didn't know he was there, Jason picked Kelsey up, kissed her and waited.

"Where is Kelsey?" With a mock roar, Sara swung around and headed for the door.

The little girl's giggle told Sara she had moved from behind the couch. She crawled to the door on all fours,
growling loudly, encouraged by Kelsey's laughter. The large
pair of shoes in the doorway brought her to an abrupt halt.

"Oops!"

Her nose was a mere four inches away from his jeans.
Sinking back on her heels, Sara put a hand up to straighten
her hair. Her gaze slowly trailed up long muscular legs and
a solid chest, slipping over a pugnacious jaw and firm lips,
till it finally stopped at Jason Graham's amused eyes.

The color rushed to her face as he said, "Hello, Sara."

"It's Kelsey's dinnertime," Mrs. Garcia announced, ap-
pearing at Jason's elbow and holding her arms out to the
child. Kelsey went to the motherly woman immediately.

As Kelsey and Mrs. Garcia disappeared into the kitchen,
Sara got to her feet. Would Jason consider this unfiancée-
like behavior, too? Feeling extremely foolish, she tugged her
cotton sweater down. Quickly, she replaced cushions and
picked up the toys in the room.

When she turned, he hadn't moved from his spot by the
door. That was unusual. Usually he sat with Kelsey while she
ate.

Jason frowned as he intercepted the quick anxious glance
Sara gave him. Since their talk in the garden on Sunday,
she'd avoided being alone with him. If Kelsey or Mrs. Garcia weren't around, she simply disappeared to her room.
When they did exchange a few words, it was clear Sara was
uneasy around him. Jason didn't care for the thought he
inspired so much fear.

"I have something for you in my study."

"F-for me?"

Jason nodded, standing aside so she had to walk past him
to get to the hall. He followed her, noticing that the loose

cotton pants and long top she wore hid most of her, as usual.

In the study, he opened the top drawer of his desk and took out a small box, placing it on the polished surface.

"See if you like it," he said.

Sara's breath caught in her throat as she picked up the jewelry box and opened it. On a bed of midnight blue velvet nestled the most beautiful ring she had ever seen. The huge marquise diamond set in white gold must have cost the earth. She knew because Claire and she had window-shopped frequently since Uncle Samuel's death. Claire loved pretending she was a serious customer, trying jewelry on and finding out how much everything cost.

Sara looked at Jason. Why was he giving her something so expensive? Everything Uncle Samuel had given her—food, a roof over her head, clothes—had cost too much in return. Obedience, work, undying gratitude.

"It's too valuable," Sara said stiffly. "I'd be afraid of damaging or losing it."

"It's what people would expect me to give my future wife," Jason said impatiently, wondering at the same time why her reaction should hurt. She was the first woman he knew who'd responded to a gift of jewelry with anger. "Try it on."

It fit her slender finger perfectly. As she looked at him, eyes round with surprise, he said, "This morning I picked up the ring you normally wear, by the kitchen sink. That's how I got your size right. The jeweler polished your ring. Here it is."

"Thank you." Sara looked at the gold filigree band as if examining it for damage before she slipped it on her right hand.

"I couldn't help noticing it has a date inside it." Jason wondered if it was her parents' wedding date.

"That's the day my father and mother met."

"What did your father do?" At last they were having some sort of normal conversation.

Nervousness welled up in Sara. The terms of the contract they had signed in his lawyer's office had emphasized that they should be completely honest with each other. "He was an engineer in the army. He was killed before I was born, when some sort of bridge he was working on collapsed."

"I see." Sympathy welled within him for her. Had her uncle taken the place of her father, or had it been hard for her growing up without one? His own long-distance relationship with his father had been one of the most difficult things Jason had endured as a child.

"There's something you should know." She wet her lips, and Jason watched some of the color drain from her face.

"What is it?"

"My f-father and my mother weren't married." The words came out in a rush. "He loved my mother and they were going to be married on his next leave, but he died."

Jason's eyes narrowed at the defiant note in her voice. Did Sara really think things like that mattered these days? He looked at her lower lip, imprisoned by her even white teeth. Obviously to her, it did.

"Why did you feel you had to tell me, Sara?"

She blushed. "It's because of the contract . . . we have to be completely honest with each other, remember?" Wiping her hands down the sides of her pants, she said, "It's also because of what you said. You expect certain things of your fiancée, and I don't know if this comes out . . . I mean . . . It's important to some people and I don't want to embarrass you in any way. . . ."

"Thank you for letting me know, Sara." A trite remark wouldn't erase the pain she obviously carried around. He knew she wouldn't be here telling him this unless someone had made her feel she was less than perfect because her parents hadn't married. "It doesn't make any difference to me."

Her startled gaze met his. She waited, as if expecting him to say something more. When he didn't, she said, "I'll take good care of your ring. Maybe the jeweler will take it back when all this is over."

Jason stared at the closed door after Sara had rushed out of the room. Diamonds certainly weren't this woman's best friend. She'd acted as if it were part of a uniform that went with the job. Restless, he reached for a paper clip and hung it on another. Sara Adams was like Mrs. Garcia's ball of yarn after a kitten had been playing with it for a while.

Tangled up, confusing, *complex*.

She was occupying more of his thoughts than he'd expected her to. The picture of her on all fours, her bottom wiggling as she played with Kelsey, flashed into his mind. Except for the games she played with Kelsey, she was such a serious, solemn thing.

He'd have to tell her he didn't want the ring back. She could keep it as a souvenir when all this was over. When she'd looked at him, her eyes had mirrored her frightened soul, reminding him more than ever of a little golden brown owl. Inexplicably he wanted to tell her he wasn't a predatory hawk.

Jason's jaw clenched. Parenting Kelsey had turned him soft. Sara Adams was a woman, and women always knew how to take care of themselves.

In the kitchen Sara quickly set the table with one place. Jason preferred eating here than in the formal dining room.

"Going out?" Mrs. Garcia asked.

Sara nodded. "Claire and I are going shopping."

It was an excuse she had just made up. Mrs. Garcia and Jason had met Claire, on Monday evening. Sara had called Claire at work to tell her all that had happened and Claire had said she'd had to come by to meet King Midas in person. Jason had surprised Sara by inviting Claire, and her son Bobby, to stay for dinner.

Claire had been dreamy-eyed about Jason ever since. Sara sighed. In spite of the fact that Claire's husband had walked out on her and her baby son, Claire still insisted on viewing every single man through rose-colored contacts.

Sara sighed again. Jason had been different yesterday evening. He'd talked easily with Claire, and had asked Bobby how he'd broken his arm. There had been none of the stern air he adopted around her.

Claire had apologized profusely for her mistake to both of them. Soon after she'd written down Sara's ad, Claire had received a call from Bobby's school saying he'd fallen and broken his arm. She'd left immediately. Her secretary had picked up the wrong ad from her desk while she was gone. Claire was guilty of changing the wording of the ad, but not for where it ended up.

Sara hadn't been able to stay angry with Claire. An honest mistake deserved understanding. She had explained Jason's proposal to Claire, who'd told her she was crazy to refuse to marry Jason Graham.

Through her new boyfriend, who worked at a Los Angeles paper, Claire had checked Jason out and given Sara a report today. His company, Graham Electronics, had placed among the ten new businesses that had done extremely well in the past twelve months. The phenomenal success of Graham Electronics was attributed to the drive and dedication of its owner and chief executive officer, Jason Graham. According to Claire, Sara had nothing to worry about.

Sara's gaze fell on the ring. Every time she looked at it she felt unsettled. Each day here was weighing her down with more and more responsibility.

Swallowing, she recalled the strange look on Jason's face when he'd given it to her. Instinct had told her he was probably remembering the time he had given his wife one. That occasion must have been the way such moments were meant to be. Passionate, tender, *indelible*.

Looking at Kelsey's curly hair, deep dimples and tawny eyes, Sara wondered if Jason's beautiful daughter looked like his wife. Rowena Harris, Jason's secretary, had come over yesterday. She'd mentioned that Diana had been a very beautiful woman. On her, the ring would have looked perfect. On Sara's thin finger, with the bitten-down nails, it looked out of place.

This house and Mrs. Garcia were new ... Sara suspected Jason had moved to Rainbow Valley because he'd been unable to bear the memories in the house he'd shared in Pasadena with his wife.

A flash of light from it drew her attention back to her ring. Jason Graham had been right when he'd said there were certain things people would expect of his fiancée. When the time came, it was up to her to prove she could deliver what was expected of her.

Chapter Three

Jason swore as he pulled into the garage on Thursday. The sight of Dee-dee's white Cadillac parked beside the curb had ignited his temper. She chose the most awkward moments to visit Kelsey. Moses had offered to get a restraining order until the court reached a decision, but Jason had turned the idea down. He didn't want to stop Dee-dee from seeing her granddaughter.

If only she'd observe the simple courtesy of calling ahead to let him know. The last time she'd come, Kelsey had been in the sandbox. Dee-dee had clucked and fussed over her as she'd changed her grimy overalls and lectured him on germs, neglect, and the dreadful state of Kelsey's wardrobe. The next day, six little designer outfits had been delivered by special messenger.

Sara. Jason's jaw tightened. He wondered what Dee-dee had made of his new fiancée. Sara would be no match for her cunning. Slamming the car door shut, he hurried into the house.

The sound of voices directed him to the family room. Throwing his briefcase on the living room couch, he pulled his tie off as he walked down the hall. His hand on the family room door, he paused, stopped by Sara's voice.

"I'm so glad you like the ring, Dee-dee. Jason surprised me with it. He's so romantic. Won't you have another brownie?"

He blinked. The light voice, the tinkly laugh, didn't sound like the Sara he knew. Neither did the quiet confidence in her voice.

"How did you meet?" Dee-dee's voice was filled with avid curiosity. "I never thought Jason would ever put someone in my darling Diana's place, but then, the person a man chooses for his daughter is different to the one he chooses for himself. All Jason cares about is Kelsey now."

Jason's hand gripped the door handle. Dee-dee must have had a new abrasive coating put on her tongue this morning at the beauty salon she visited regularly.

"A friend got us together by accident." That light, tinkly laugh again gave no indication that Dee-dee's barbs were hitting home. "It all happened so quickly. One look and we both knew we were in love."

Jason pushed the door open. He had to make sure the person in the family room was the Sara Adams he'd employed.

The scene in the room stopped him short. Kelsey's building blocks were all over the floor. Sara and Dee-dee were on the carpet helping his daughter build a huge tower, and behind Dee-dee was a box that held a doll as large as Kelsey. Jason drew in a long breath. He hated the gifts Dee-dee brought Kelsey.

"Hi, sweetheart," he said quietly, dropping a kiss on the top of Kelsey's head. Crouching beside his daughter, he looked at Sara.

Her hair was still tied back, but in place of her normal uniform of loose sweaters and long pants or skirts, she wore a snug red top with a scooped neck and jeans. If it wasn't for the usual flicker of nervousness he glimpsed as their gazes met, he would have thought this was Sara's twin. "Hello, Sara, Dee-dee."

"Jason, darling! What a surprise to see you here so early." He stared at Sara, but the shocks weren't over yet. She knelt, placed her arms around his neck and dropped a kiss full on his lips, following it up with another quick one, as if she couldn't help herself. Only he saw the embarrassment in her eyes, felt the way her arms trembled as she smiled at him. Behind him, Kelsey clapped her hands and giggled approval of the new game.

As if it were something she did all the time, Sara tenderly placed the palm of her hand against his cheek.

"Dee-dee and I have been getting to know each other." Sara kept her face turned toward him, so Dee-dee wouldn't see the way her mouth trembled. "Maybe we can all go out to lunch now that you're here."

Jason nodded, unable to say a word. He was still pole-axed by Sara's transformation, by the way her soft mouth had felt against his.

"I have to leave." Dee-dee sniffed as she got to her feet. "I just came over to say goodbye to Kelsey. It was a good thing I did. The poor child was out in the sandbox again, in a dreadful, filthy state."

Jason felt Sara stiffen. As she moved away from him, he placed an arm around her waist to keep her by his side. "Being out in the fresh air is good for Kelsey. The sand in the box is clean, and getting that kind of dirty hasn't killed any kid yet."

Something in Jason's tone must have been warning enough because Dee-dee decided to change the subject.

"Well, I've brought her something she can play with indoors. I hear you're leaving Sunday night. How long are you going to be away for this time?"

"Six weeks."

"All this traveling is hard on Kelsey. I might take a trip to London, in the next couple of weeks. I want to watch the Trooping of the Color this year."

Check he wasn't neglecting his own daughter, was more like it. Jason's temper rose. "Dee-dee—" he began, when Sara interrupted.

"We'll look forward to your visit."

Dee-dee looked taken aback. "You're going to London, too?"

"Of course." Jason turned and dropped a kiss on the top of Sara's head. Her hair smelled nice. "Sara and Kelsey are getting to know each other."

Dee-dee sniffed again. "See you hire some good help when you get there. I won't have my granddaughter neglected, just because your head is in the clouds."

Bending, she gave Kelsey a hug and a kiss, and turned away without a word to him. Jason fumed as Sara walked Dee-dee to the door.

"Did she call before she came?" he asked angrily when Sara returned.

She hesitated by the door, as if wondering whether to come in.

"No." Sara began to put the blocks into the toy chest.

"She always does that," he said angrily.

"She loves Kelsey."

Jason stared at her in exasperation. Whose side was Sara Adams on, anyway? She'd switched back to her normal role; avoiding his eyes, working as if he were a slave driver with an invisible whip in his hands.

As she stood by the window stacking the blocks, Jason's thoughts distracted him from his anger for the space of one minute. The jeans clung to the curves of her hips and outlined her long, slender legs. The top hugged her breasts, its neckline giving him a glimpse of her delicate collarbone. The coltish grace of her body was very attractive. Something stirred within him and he frowned, trying to concentrate on the matter at hand.

"I don't want you encouraging her."

"No one can stop her. Sara did her best." Jason stared at the housekeeper who stood in the door of the family room. The woman who rarely talked except for "Yes, Mr. Graham," "No, Mr. Graham," sounded like a tigress defending her cub. "My eyes almost fell out of my head the way you handled Mrs. Smythe. You were great, Sara. Come, Kelsey, it's lunchtime."

The words reminded him he hadn't thanked Sara for the way she'd risen to the occasion. Her chameleonlike change had unsettled him. Which was the real Sara? The quiet woman who stood holding a cushion as if it were a shield, or the woman who had greeted him in front of Dee-dee?

Their gazes tangled, and Jason watched the color stain her face and neck. He knew they were both thinking of the kiss.

Could he have been wrong about her?

"I used to love acting in school, and I took part in the annual play every year." Sara made it all sound very simple and straightforward. "Dee-dee was very suspicious. I knew it would take a great deal to convince her that we were really in love."

"You were convincing," Jason said grimly. She'd certainly convinced *him* she was a great actress.

"I just cast myself in the role of loving fiancée, that's all. Television gives one plenty of ideas how to act that out. I'm sorry if anything I did upset you."

Jason knew she sensed his tension. What she didn't know was that he was angry with Dee-dee, not her.

"You said yourself part of my job was not to let anyone guess the engagement wasn't real," Sara reminded him. "You also said that as long as we handled these awkward moments professionally, everything would be fine."

He recalled the silken embrace of her arms, the soft whisper of her untried mouth against his. For an instant he'd been wrapped in the subtle scent of jasmine. Jason's heartbeat quickened at the memory.

For a few seconds he was tempted to reach for Sara Adams and show her what a real kiss was like. The fact he'd responded to her inexperienced touch, however, unsettled him. He'd been out with a couple of women since Diana's death, but he might as well have saved himself the trouble. Their kisses had left him unmoved, convincing him the armor he'd donned since Diana couldn't be penetrated.

Sara Adams's performance had just caught him by surprise. Shock was the only reason the kiss had disturbed him. The next time he would be more prepared.

"I stopped by to pick up a couple of disks," he said. "I'd better get back to the office."

Work would help his emotions settle.

At the door he stopped and looked back at Sara. She still stood by the toy chest, hugging the cushion to her, looking like a child who'd been snubbed. Jason's jaw clenched.

"You did great, Sara," he said reluctantly. "Thanks."

Sara put the cushion down as the door closed. Putting a hand up, she ran a finger over her lips. Had she gone overboard in her attempt to convince Dee-dee that she and Jason were really an item?

The woman's incredulous reception of the news that she was Jason's fiancée and her probing questions had made Sara realize the true extent of what Jason was up against.

A stream of double-edged remarks about Jason being a poor father had goaded Sara's building anger. The kiss had stemmed from her conviction that only her actions would convince Dee-dee.

She'd only been doing her job. Hadn't she?

Sara tugged the neckline of the dark red clingy top Claire had given her at Christmas. She'd never had the courage to wear it before. She'd never felt more self-conscious as when Jason's gaze had swept over her.

She hoped Dee-dee wouldn't visit often. How did one handle hugs, kisses and close encounters of the physical kind professionally? She didn't know. The only kisses Sara could recall were the harmless ones she'd exchanged with a boy in her high school class. After Mom's death, Uncle Samuel's demands and attitude had made dating impossible.

Sara's palm tingled as she recalled the firm, smooth feel of Jason's skin. His mouth had been very warm, very firm. The pressure of it against hers had surprised her. She hadn't been able to withdraw quickly, because that would have made Dee-dee suspicious, but she hadn't expected Jason's mouth to open, or for his tongue to paint a searing line of heat along her lips.

Recollection lit a spark in the pit of her stomach that moved up and into her breasts. It was the first time Sara Adams had really been kissed by a man.

It was hard to believe she was on a flight to England, just as it was hard to believe everything that had happened since her first meeting with Jason nine days ago. Sara turned her hand. In the glow from the overhead light above her seat, the diamond in her mock-engagement ring seemed to release hidden fires.

The executive-class cabin they were in was the last word in comfort. Between her seat and Jason's was Kelsey's empty seat. The airline crib attached to the cabin wall in front of their seats held the sleeping cherub.

She hadn't seen much of Jason since his mother-in-law's visit. Not that she minded, Sara told herself quickly. Mrs. Harris had discussed the arrangements for their trip with Sara. Jason and Kelsey had a complete set of clothes in the London apartment that overlooked Hyde Park, she'd said, so there was no need to pack anything for Kelsey, except a carry-on bag and her latest favorite toy.

According to Mrs. Harris, the "flat," as she called the apartment in London, was close to the shops, theaters and everything else that made London interesting.

It had all sounded very grand, but would Kelsey be happy there? Sara wondered if there was any truth in Dee-dee's accusation about Kelsey's unsettled life having a detrimental effect on her progress. Was Kelsey going to be upset by this trip? So far, Sara and she had gotten on very well. Gradually Sara had taken over doing everything for Kelsey from Mrs. Garcia. The little girl was very sweet and very intelligent. She understood everything that was said to her, proving there was nothing really wrong with her.

Sara had packed her own things in the new suitcase Mrs. Garcia had brought to her room.

"Mr. Graham wants you to use this," she'd said.

Mrs. Garcia wouldn't be there when they returned. Her daughter in Sacramento was having a baby, and the housekeeper was moving there to live close to her. Sara had grown to like the quiet woman with the shining black eyes who had insisted she rub an aloe vera cream into her hands every day to soften the dry, chapped skin.

Sara closed her eyes as Jason turned his head in her direction. He'd told her to catch some sleep after dinner had been served, but she was too restless to sleep.

The thought she'd never have need of Uncle Samuel's charity now, undid another tie to the past. By the time this job was over, she would have enough money to get her own apartment.

Sara's face was turned away from him, so he couldn't tell if her eyes were open, but Jason knew she was still awake. A blue airline blanket covered her from neck to toe, hiding the jeans, T-shirt and denim jacket she'd worn to travel in.

"Can't sleep?" He pushed the bell that would summon the air hostess.

She turned toward him. "I'm sorry if I disturbed you."

He'd bet a year's income that he couldn't spend five minutes in Sara Adams's company without hearing some sort of an apology. She had taken great care not to be alone with him since Dee-dee's visit. When she *was* around him she still acted like a new recruit before an army sergeant.

"Can I help you, sir?" The air hostess smiled at him.

"A glass of warm milk with a tablespoon of brandy for my fiancée, please."

He watched Sara's eyes widen.

"It will help you fall asleep."

"What if Kelsey wakes up and I don't hear her?"

She took her responsibilities as seriously as she took everything else. Rowena had told him she'd never met anyone as determined to be perfect as Sara. Very little impressed his secretary, but after two visits with Sara, she had joined the Sara Adams fan club, of which Moses and Mrs. Garcia were already members.

"There you go." The air hostess returned, flipping Sara's tray down and placing a glass on it.

"Kelsey's just gone down," Jason told her when Sara made no move to pick up the glass. "She's a veteran traveler. I doubt if she'll wake up till we reach Heathrow, but I'll keep an eye on her. I have work to do. Try the milk, Sara."

In the overhead light, Jason Graham's eyes looked inky and very compelling. Sara sipped the milk cautiously, reminded of Claire's last comment at the airport.

Jason Graham's eyes could beam a woman up to heaven. Are you blind, Sara?

She wasn't blind, but Jason Graham was her employer. He'd made it very clear he didn't want any complications. Sara didn't think he would hesitate firing her if he thought for one minute that she would cause him any trouble. Not, she told herself quickly, that she had the slightest wish to do anything like that. She didn't want Jason Graham to have any cause for complaint. This job was very important to her.

Jason Graham was a very tough man with room for only one female in his life, his daughter, Kelsey. Which reminded Sara of what she had to say.

"There's something I'd like to discuss with you."

Jason capped the pen he was using and looked at her. "Yes?"

Sara cleared her throat. The yes hadn't been very encouraging. "It's about Kelsey."

"What about her?" She had his complete attention now.

Sara wished she'd talked to him before she'd drunk the milk. It felt like a curdled lump in her throat. "It's about *you* and Kelsey."

"What about me and Kelsey?"

Sara drew a deep breath and let the words fly. "You...you do a lot of things for her...bathe her and feed her and put her to sleep...but you don't play with her."

She closed her eyes and waited for the anger. He hadn't liked Dee-dee's criticism of his daughter and he wasn't going to like this.

The silence forced Sara to open her eyes. "I'm only telling you this because the contract said we had to be completely honest with each other...." Her voice trailed away. She'd just emptied her personal tank of courage.

"Go on, Sara." The tightness was back around his mouth. As she watched, he put a hand up and rubbed it across his forehead as if his head hurt.

"It's great the way you look after Kelsey," she said quickly. "I mean, I've seen fathers at the preschool who didn't know which foot their kids' shoes went on, or how to do up their jackets. You're super in that department, but it's important to do fun things together, too. Shared laughter creates an important bond."

Jason looked at the paperwork on his tray table. He was going over what might turn out to be a multimillion-dollar contract. He had a custody case on his hands, and a dozen other problems that went with running a company. About to tell Sara this wasn't the time to lay a guilt trip on him, he looked at her. The quiver of her mouth, the look in her eyes, changed his mind. She was very serious.

"And I'm falling short in that department, am I?"

"Yes, unless you count Kelsey's bath time. I know you both enjoy that, but Kelsey needs more. Mrs. Garcia used to take her out on the swings, and I play games with her. You should, too."

Jason thought of the games Sara played with his daughter. She never had a problem romping on the floor with Kelsey. Yesterday they'd both been having a mock cushion fight when he'd come home.

"You'll have to show me how to play, Sara."

"You've got to set a time aside for playing every day. Ideally, it should be the same time every day."

"I'm going to be very busy the first week in London, but after that I can work something out."

"Good. I'll show you a few simple games you can start with. You'll get the hang of it. I make up games sometimes. It isn't too difficult, you know."

"I hope not." Jason reached over and switched off the light over Sara's seat. "Now we've settled that, try and get some sleep, Sara."

Sara looked out the window at the dripping rain that hadn't stopped since they'd arrived. So much for an English summer. Something about the relentless tap-tap-tap of heavy raindrops found an echo in the restlessness deep inside her. It wasn't supposed to rain in June. She wasn't supposed to feel so unsettled.

You've gotten everything you wanted. A job, a new life. What's wrong with you?

The penthouse apartment was incredibly spacious. A living cum dining room, a kitchen with an adjoining laundry room. Four bedrooms with attached bathrooms, maid's quarters. The master bedroom that Jason used even had an area that he'd set up as his home office—complete with computer, fax machine and private telephone line.

He must be very busy, because she hadn't seen him once in the two days since they'd settled in after landing at Heathrow Monday morning. He'd come in late last night, and she'd heard him moving around. Kelsey had woken up around midnight and had stayed up till 4:00 a.m. Sara had heard Jason talking and playing with his daughter until Kelsey had fallen asleep again. She'd purposely stayed in her room, because Jason had made it very clear that as far as he was concerned he wanted to do everything for Kelsey when he was around.

Right now Kelsey was fast asleep in the bedroom between Sara's and Jason's. The move hadn't upset her, neither had their new surroundings...she was as happy here as she'd been in Rainbow Valley. The refrigerator and pantry were well stocked, and caring for herself and Kelsey was super-easy in the luxury apartment. So there was no accounting for this strange feeling.

Sara turned the stereo up just slightly, so that the sounds of the symphony would drown out the noise of the rain. Returning to the couch, she picked up a cushion. Hugging it, she decided she was just unsettled because she had nothing to do. Kelsey's body clock still hadn't tuned in to London time, so she slept a great deal, whereas Sara's jet lag was beginning to wear off and she wasn't used to having so much time on her hands.

She'd explored every inch of the apartment, and found evidence of what a great dad Jason was. Kelsey's closet held an identical set of clothes to the ones she wore in California and the toys were the same ones she played with back home. The child's bedroom here even had the same clown wallpaper as the one in Rainbow Valley. Buying two of everything couldn't be cheap, but Sara knew money was the least of Jason Graham's concerns. Making the changes as easy as possible for his little girl was all that mattered.

The heavy carryon she'd seen him taking on board the plane had contained Kelsey's clothes, her favorite soups and baby jars of fruit. He'd told her he preferred to make sure Kelsey's menu wouldn't be too different in the first week.

Jason Graham deserved to be named International Father of the Year, if there was such a title around.

Sara drew her knees up to her chest and wrapped her arms around them, telling herself for the tenth time that day that she was lucky to have gotten this job. Her whole life had changed. It was as if the patron saint of employment had decided she needed a break.

At times the thought that nothing really was different nagged at Sara's mind. Except for Jason Graham, she didn't know anyone in England. If she wanted to go out by herself, she wouldn't know where to go, or what to do. She felt very much tied to him, the way she had felt tied to Uncle Samuel.

There was one major difference, though. Uncle Samuel had been verbally abusive. His constant put-downs were a sharp contrast to Jason, who hardly said anything.

Leaning her head against the back of the couch, Sara told herself to stop imagining Jason Graham as a jailer. As soon as it was sunny, she would put Kelsey in a stroller and they would take long walks in the park she could see from the bedroom window. In her time off, she would take a guided bus tour of London, get to know her way around.

Jason pushed the elevator button. It was good to be home early, to know that Kelsey was so happy with Sara that he'd be able to get back to work after the evening meal.

Buying this apartment five months ago, when he'd realized he was going to need a permanent base in London, had been a smart move. He'd heard of it through his friend, Peter Wilton.

A shrewd businessman had bought an old house in Bayswater from his noble but poor relative, torn it down, and put up a high-rise apartment building that he'd named The Towers. On a quiet street, a stone's throw away from Hyde Park, the apartment was ideally located.

The Towers was a wonderfully planned building. It had everything anyone wanted right here. The ground floor had an assortment of shops, a deli, a health club and a beauty parlor. The apartments were separated from the shopping arcade by double-glass doors; a doorman also served as security officer.

As he got out of the elevator, Jason wondered how Sara and Kelsey had spent the day. The past two days had been hectic, but now he'd organized his schedule so that he'd be able to leave the office by four each afternoon.

Moving his briefcase to his other hand, he dug into his right pocket for the key to the apartment. The first thing Jason noticed as he opened the door was Sara curled up in a corner of the couch, fast asleep. For a moment he just stood and stared at her. He hadn't seen her since the day they'd arrived. Each night she'd left a note in the kitchen that there was dinner in the refrigerator for him in case he was hungry.

He wondered if she was bored in the apartment. With her hand tucked under her cheek, she looked very young and very innocent and he was suddenly reminded of the way her head had felt against his shoulder in the aircraft. When she'd fallen asleep, he'd moved the two armrests out of the way and shifted into Kelsey's seat, so Sara would have a place to rest her head. Did she know she'd slept like that?

From the utility room off the kitchen, the dryer made a sound, indicating the drying cycle was complete. Getting the clothes out and folding them was a chore he'd done often. He was halfway through it when he realized something. Sara's nightgowns were faded and darned, her underwear plain. He frowned. He'd thought everyone threw away their clothes as soon as they got holes in them.

Was Sara so poor that she had to mend her clothes until there was barely anything left to mend?

He thought of the box she'd packed her things in, of the worn handbag she carried around. The house Sara had lived in was in a good area of Rainbow Valley. Why had she been treated like a poor relation? Rowena had made an odd remark after she'd met Sara. *I don't care how rich the uncle was. Miss Adams hasn't had an easy life.*

Twin prongs of guilt and determination gripped him. He should have done something about her clothes before now. He would attend to it in the next twenty-four hours.

He was folding the last item in the basket when Sara came awake with a start. The moment she saw him, panic overtook her face. The glance she cast the clock on the mantel was frantic.

"I didn't mean to fall asleep. I'll have dinner ready in a jiffy. Would you like some coffee in the meantime?"

Jason caught her arm just as she sprang off the couch and turned toward the kitchen.

"Where's the fire?" Had someone told Sara he expected to be waited on hand and foot? "Dinner can wait. How was your day?"

She glanced at the large brown laundry basket, her eyes widening, the color on her face deepening. "You didn't have to fold the clothes. I would have done that. Kelsey's body is still on California time, so I have almost nothing to do."

"It usually takes a week for her to adjust." Ignoring the look she cast the door, Jason firmly steered Sara back to the couch. "Are you bored?"

"Of course not." She looked as if he'd suggested something outrageous. "I meant to have dinner ready. I just don't know how I fell asleep. I'm sorry."

"Would you like to have a drink?"

"No, thank you." She looked toward the kitchen as if wondering how she could get there. "Kelsey is fine. She's eating well and we played a couple of games before she got sleepy. She loves her plastic building set."

"I'm sure Kelsey had a good time today," Jason said, doggedly. "I asked how *your* day was."

Sara's surprise showed plainly as she said, "Fine. Just fine."

"I want the truth. It can't be easy for you being cooped up in here with a small child." Diana had hated the brief times she'd spent alone with Kelsey.

Sara's eyes opened wide. "I enjoy caring for Kelsey."

Jason's eyes narrowed. Was she afraid to tell him how she really felt? "I've contacted an agency to provide us with a nanny and a maid. You'll have more free time once they get here."

Dismay flashed across Sara's face. "There's no need to hire anyone else," she said earnestly. "You're spending too much money on me as it is. I love being with Kelsey, and when she's napping, I can clean the place and cook the evening meal. I only fell asleep today because of the rain. I'm sorry."

The soft, absolutely unnecessary apology unleashed a primitive anger within Jason. "Sara, you are *not* my personal slave. All this cooking, washing up, caring for Kelsey, isn't your job. You were hired to be my fiancée, nothing else."

Sara kept quiet. There was no sense arguing with the man now. When he'd eaten, he'd be in a better mood, and she would talk to him again then.

Apparently Jason wasn't on the same wavelength as she was because he said, "The agency's sending five women over tomorrow, starting at two. They all come highly recommended and have experience caring for children. I told the agency we want to hire a maid and a housekeeper-nanny type."

"Are you going to be here to interview them?"

Jason looked surprised. "No. I thought you'd take care of that for me."

"Me?" Sara blurted, petrified by the idea. She'd never even interviewed a garden bug. "I wouldn't know what to say to those women."

"There's a first time for everything, isn't there?"

Sara stared at him. Jason seemed to take it for granted she'd do it. That she *could* do it.

Miserable, she watched as he reached under the bar counter and took out a bag of potato chips. Opening the bag, he filled two glass dishes with the chips, and handed her one as he seated himself in the chair opposite her.

"It isn't so very complex. You make a list of things you think are most important, and ask the women questions about their experience."

Sara stared at the bowl. How could he trust her with something so important as choosing the right person to take care of Kelsey? Uncle Samuel had always said that the only thing she could be trusted to do was to make a complete mess of everything.

Jason seemed to guess her uneasiness, because he asked quietly, "What kind of person do you think Kelsey needs, Sara?"

"Someone who will travel with you between the States and England. Someone who is willing to stay with you for the next five to ten years."

"See?" he said encouragingly. "You're already on the right track. There's nothing to it."

Cold chilled her from the inside out. What if she chose the wrong person for Kelsey?

Jason got to his feet, bowl of chips in hand. "I'm going to get Kelsey up and then if you'll keep an eye on her, I'll cook dinner. Wait till you try my Chinese fried rice."

"Cooking's my job," Sara protested, getting off the couch.

The hand he placed on her shoulder had her sinking back into the couch. Her gaze rested on his hand and then traced a path up his arm to his face. The dark blue shirt he'd worn with his gray suit made his eyes look more hypnotic than ever.

"Why?" His tone and analytical look confused her as did his closeness.

"What do you mean, why? I haven't done a thing all day."

"Why is cooking and doing the laundry your job? Did Moses include it as part of the contract we signed?"

"Of course not. It's just that I haven't done a thing all day and you've been working so hard...." And Uncle Samuel had always made it very clear that household chores were a woman's job.

"I want you to sit here and plan out your new routine."

"R-routine?" His hand on her shoulder pumped heat and chaos directly to her brain.

"Once we get the staff, you'll be able to call your time your own. There's a health club and a beauty parlor in this building, and the bus stop and taxi stands are a block away. The subway station's close by, too. I have a couple of guidebooks I'll dig out for you. You can go shopping, tour London, do anything you feel like."

Sara stared at him as if she didn't have the power to look away. True, she'd wanted some freedom; she just hadn't expected to have it handed to her in one big package marked Now.

"Did Rowena give you a couple of charge cards?"

"Yes." They were tucked safely away in the back flap of her suitcase. Sara couldn't imagine using someone else's line of credit.

"Would you like that?"

"Like what?" she asked blankly.

"Shopping, sight-seeing, spending time at the health club?"

"I don't know," she said. It was hard to tune in to the picture Jason Graham seemed to have of her in his mind. "I've never done those things before."

He masked his surprise quickly. "What are your interests, Sara?"

She blinked, thinking of the journal hidden in her suitcase. No one except Claire knew about the essays and poetry she liked to write.

"I like reading, and I took a few courses in journalism once." Tense, she waited for Jason Graham's reaction. Uncle Samuel had always said she was as dull as ditch water, without talent for anything except cleaning and cooking.

"You'll enjoy visiting the library in the British Museum, then. The London Library in St. James Square is very good, too, and then there are all the bookstores on Charing Cross Road. Some of them invite authors and poets to read their work there. You might enjoy attending something like that."

It was so exactly what she would like that Sara held her breath for a second. She didn't know if it was Jason's hand on her shoulder or his words that had confusion spilling into her system.

"Maybe," she said cautiously. "But it's going to take a while for Kelsey to get used to someone new. I'm not going to leave her with a couple of strangers right away."

Jason's hand tightened on her shoulder. It had never bothered Diana to leave Kelsey with anyone. Why should Sara feel so responsible for her?

Unless it was all an act, like the role she'd assumed when Dee-dee had come over. His eyes narrowed. Women were good at playing a part. Diana had been so different before they'd married. It had taken exactly two weeks *after* they were married for Jason to realize that Diana had seen him as her ticket up in the world. He was to be groomed for a role she'd had in mind, so she could rub shoulders with the uppermost crust of society. The realities of becoming a mother had been something she'd never been able to handle.

You tricked me into getting pregnant, and now you're forcing me to play mother, as you conceive the role should be played. I won't do it, Jason, do you hear?

As he recalled Diana's favorite two lines, Jason's hand fell to his side. He wasn't going to be taken in again.

"Kelsey will be fine with whoever we hire," he said abruptly. "Just make sure you find something to keep yourself occupied. I don't have the time or inclination to entertain you."

He strode from the room, unaware that Sara was staring open-mouthed after him.

Chapter Four

Twenty-four hours later Sara was positive she should not have agreed to interview the applicants. She'd spent fifteen minutes talking to each woman, and they all seemed to have perfect qualifications. After they'd gone, she pored over the notes she'd made as she'd talked to them, wondering why her uneasiness had increased with each meeting.

The responsibility of making the best choice for Kelsey rested heavily on her shoulders. The little girl was too solemn for her age. Her insecurity was apparent in the way she clung to Jason. Whoever took care of her had to build up Kelsey's confidence, be a stable factor in the little girl's constantly changing world.

Would Jason be annoyed that she'd decided none of the women seen today were suitable? Ten days with Kelsey hardly gave her the right to make arbitrary decisions. It was just that something was missing. Sara hoped she would be able to identify the ''something'' by the time Jason came home, so she could give him a concrete reason for her decision. Biting her lip, Sara went over her notes.

The key turning in the lock a little while later startled her. A glance at her wristwatch showed it was only four-fifteen. Kelsey was still asleep, and she hadn't started dinner.

"Hi!" Jason put his briefcase down, placing a large box on the kitchen table.

"I'm afraid I wasn't paying attention to the time." She was beginning to sound like a recording. "I'll get Kelsey up, and start dinner right away. It won't be long. Why don't you sit down and relax?"

As Jason loosened his tie and undid the top button of the blue shirt he wore, Sara stared at his big hands with the lean, strong fingers. He caught her gaze and asked, "Do I have an invisible sign around my neck that reads, Vicious When Hungry, or something like that?"

Sara stared at the quirk of his mouth. He was laughing at her? Strange, she hadn't paid any attention to that beautiful, mobile mouth before. A sudden, dizzying warmth flooded her as she continued to look at it.

"Sit down and tell me about your day." Jason filled the electric kettle with water and plugged it in.

"I—I'll get Kelsey up." She had to get away, to let the funny feeling in the pit of her stomach settle.

He looked at his watch. "Another half hour's sleep won't hurt Kelsey. She can stay up with me tonight. I've brought some work home. How did those interviews go?"

"I didn't like any of them."

The defiant way she said the words caught Jason's attention. Setting two mugs on the counter, he turned and looked at her. "Oh?"

"I don't know much about these things, but none of those women felt right for Kelsey."

Her color was high. The way she clenched the pen in her hand made her knuckles show up white. Something had ruffled the little owl's feathers.

"What type do you think will be the right one for her?" Pouring hot water into the mugs, he added tea bags.

"She needs someone who will cuddle her and play with her. Someone who won't mind getting down on the rug and playing with her every now and then."

"And these women don't do those things?"

He watched Sara lift a notepad from the table and flick through the pages. "The first woman talked of discipline, the second said she didn't like anyone interfering in her routine, the third said she'd worked for an earl and knew how important manners were, the fourth and fifth looked as if their clothes had been starched with them inside."

Jason fought the urge to laugh. Sara's serious expression told him now wasn't a good time.

"That will never do," he said in a voice that sounded choked.

Sara nodded. "Kelsey doesn't have to be the perfect child, only a happy one. She doesn't need someone to fill her life with rules and manners and discipline. Those things are important, but what Kelsey needs first is love. None of these women looked capable of loving her."

Taken aback, Jason stared at Sara as she flipped the pages of the pad. She'd made notes on each woman?

"Most important of all, she needs someone who can tell her stories. Not one of the applicants mentioned reading to their charges, or telling them stories."

The indignant note in her voice made the corner of Jason's mouth lift.

"And stories are important?" he asked as he brought the mugs to the kitchen table.

"Of course," Sara said quickly. "Very important. They stretch the mind, help the imagination to grow."

Jason stared at Sara, caught up in the sheer poetry of her words. "I heard the story you told Kelsey last night."

"You did?" She wondered if the intercom system had been left on in Kelsey's bedroom.

"I was on the balcony after the rain stopped, and her bedroom window was open, so I sat down and listened. You're a wonderful storyteller, Sara."

She felt herself blush. All four bedrooms opened onto a balcony that stretched the length of the apartment. She hadn't thought Jason would be out there. Her story had been a simple made-up tale about a goose that had decided to go to London on business, and had taken his little gosling along with him. "Sometimes kids understand a situation better when they hear or read about it in the form of a story."

Sara sipped her tea cautiously. Had Jason been upset by the fact that in her story the gosling hadn't started talking? The story had ended with the gosling opening its bill and yelling, "Daddy!" much to everyone's delight.

Jason stood, and Sara got to her feet, as well. "Dinner—" she began, when he interrupted.

"Don't move from there. I'm going to get Kelsey up, and the three of us are going out for fish-and-chips. There's a place just around the corner that makes the best fish-and-chips you've ever tasted."

"We don't have to go out today," Sara protested. "You cooked yesterday. I'll fix a meal in no time. You must be tired after the long hours you've worked."

Jason didn't know who'd made the rules Sara lived by, but it was time she learned some new ones. The finger he placed on her lips was the best way he could think of to stop her protests.

"A walk helps me relax after a day at work," he told her. "No more arguing. Open the box while I get Kelsey up."

When he'd disappeared in the direction of Kelsey's bedroom, Sara touched her lips. The spot where Jason's finger had rested burned. Strange as it sounded, she hadn't wanted him to remove his hand. A part of her still ached in protest that the contact had been nothing more than cursory.

Sara blinked. What on earth was wrong with her? Had being cooped up in the apartment made her lose her perspective on the situation? Jason Graham was her *employer*, and he'd warned her in no uncertain terms that he wouldn't tolerate any familiarity.

Trying to shake off the warm sensation, Sara stared at the shiny gray-and-silver striped box. Reaching out, she slipped off the bow and lifted the lid. Her heart jumped when she moved the pink tissue aside. The incredibly delicate silk and lace undies were in her size. There were six matching sets in jewel colors. Next she pulled out two teddies that made her blush. It seemed as if they'd reveal more than they would cover. Under everything were two nightgowns with matching robes. Ribbon, soft lace and delicate embroidery combined to make the garments incredibly beautiful.

The brown paper bag in the corner of the box looked like a lunch bag. Sara opened it and her face flamed as she took out a set of her own underwear. It didn't take a genius to know how Jason Graham had guessed her size.

Sara dropped everything back and replaced the lid as if the box contained a venomous snake. Her cheeks burned with embarrassment. Why had he done this?

"Do you like them?" He came in, a sleepy Kelsey still resting her head on his shoulder.

"Why did you get them?"

His eyes narrowed at her tone. "Why not? I thought you needed a few new things and I just happened to pass a shop at lunchtime."

It came to her in a flash. He'd seen her things the day he'd folded the laundry and he'd felt sorry for her. Sara thought she'd dissolve into a big puddle of embarrassment.

"I don't need them," she said stiffly.

The anger in her voice reminded him of the day he'd given her the ring. Didn't the woman like anything? He looked at her face and got his answer. Sara was embarrassed by *what* he'd gotten her.

"If it makes you feel better, I didn't pick the things out myself. I gave one of the salesclerks your things and told her to put in whatever you might need, and then I picked up the box after lunch."

That did make her feel slightly better. "If you'll tell me where you got them from, I'll return the things for you."

"It's a very small gift, Sara. I want you to keep them."

"I never accept charity, Mr. Graham."

What made her think he was offering any? He thought of his earlier assumption that Sara Adams might be badly off. He'd been like that when he'd first started his company, too poor to afford things, too proud to let anyone guess.

Putting Kelsey in her chair, Jason handed her the covered plastic cup he'd filled with juice, and then took the chair next to Sara. "Look, it's no big deal, okay? I just happened to notice you needed a few new things and I got them for you." She didn't look at him, and exasperation made him say, "I don't want whoever we hire to wonder why my fiancée is wearing darned clothes."

Sara's face burned. She hadn't thought of it from that angle. Pushing her chair back, she stood, forcing herself to look at Jason. If it was part of her job, she would accept the gift. "I'm sorry I didn't think about that myself."

The feeling he'd done something wrong, that to Sara all this *was* a big deal, bothered Jason. She'd left the room as if wearing the new things was a chore she couldn't avoid.

He looked at Kelsey, who was watching him over the rim of her cup. "Women!" he said with a shrug. "Who can understand them?"

Kelsey put her empty cup on the table, shrugged her shoulders exactly as her father had, and smiled.

Jason picked her up. "Come here, punkin," he said. "We have to think up a few games between us. Think you'll like to play horsey?"

Peter Wilton, a man he'd done his masters with in northern California, had told him today that his son loved being carried around on his dad's shoulders. Jason was going to try it with Kelsey.

In her room, Sara put the box on her bed and stared at it.

Jason Graham had won this round. Something about him warned Sara that he would win every round he wanted to. Sara wished she had enough money to offer to pay for the things, but she didn't. The box alone looked as if it might cost two weeks' salary. Her heart sank as some of the implications of being Jason's temporary fiancée dawned on her. It wasn't only everything she was, it was also everything she had, that would have to reflect her new station in life.

She took the lid off the box again and lifted the things out. To do her job well, she would have to act as if it were no big deal to her, as well. She would have to bury her qualms and learn to fit into Jason's world, so she wouldn't let him down.

All of a sudden Sara felt scared...as if she were being carried out of her depth by strong, dangerous currents to an area where the things expected of her would be those she couldn't give.

Had she bitten off more than she could chew?

Laughter greeted Jason as he unlocked the front door the next day. Sara and Kelsey sat on the carpet, surrounded by dolls and tiny garments. The flames of the gas fire picked up gold highlights in Sara's hair.

She looked up and smiled at him. It was the first smile that held no trace of shyness and Jason was surprised by the tug of response inside him.

"I found the perfect pair," she said as Kelsey ran to him and wrapped her arms around his legs.

"You did?" His expression didn't give away the fact that the agency had already told him what had happened. Lifting Kelsey, he put her up on his shoulders.

"It's a couple really, Marge and Ed Binty. They've seen twenty years of domestic service, was how they put it. Between them they'll cook, clean and care for Kelsey. They have passports and a work permit. They've traveled all over the world with an English couple and their two children, who are teenagers now. The Bintys say they love visiting new places and it doesn't matter to them where they live."

She had drawn her knees up to her chest, and was staring into the gas fire.

"But do they tell stories?" Jason teased.

Sara nodded seriously. "She and her husband both do. They have six grandchildren. I know Kelsey won't lack for hugs and kisses and kindness with them. If it's all right with you, they can start Monday."

"That's fine." It was strange how he trusted Sara's choice, especially when he'd been afraid to leave Kelsey in the same room with her own mother, when Diana had been drinking.

"There's something you should know about them." Sara bit her lip.

"What's that, Sara?"

"They're not like the other women the agency sent out. Those women were more . . . more professional-looking and spoke the Queen's English. The Bintys are ordinary, like me. They're from Yorkshire and their accents are a bit different."

Jason's jaw clenched. Why did she always expect the worst of him? "I have no problem with ordinary people, Sara. Tell them they can start right away."

"Don't you want to meet them, decide for yourself?"

"No, Sara. I trust your judgment."

"Why?" Her gaze searched his face for an answer.

"Because in the last three years, I've never thought of Kelsey needing love and stories. I've just hired someone who would take care of her. You've shown me what's really important."

Sara blushed, then looked as if she was going to cry. With a muttered "Excuse me," she dashed from the room. Jason wondered what he'd said to upset her now. Kelsey patted his head and he said, "Hold on now. Daddy's ready to go."

His version of a gallop through the dining area and kitchen had Kelsey in splits of laughter that warmed him all the way through.

"I had something in my eye," Sara said, when she came back to the living room.

Sure, and he was the next heir to the throne. Jason decided to let it pass for the time being. He had something else on his mind right now. Sitting down, he let Kelsey tumble off his shoulders onto the couch. "One of my business colleagues and his wife have invited us out for dinner any day you feel like it."

"I can't leave Kelsey."

She didn't want to go to any parties with him. She was too afraid of letting him down. The way he'd acted about her underthings told Sara her black skirt and pink blouse wouldn't do for these occasions.

"Kelsey won't be alone. The Bintys will be here. You can even put her to bed before we leave."

Sara bit her lip and stared into the fire. Nervousness mingled with the fear that circled her heart. She couldn't do it.

"What's the matter, Sara? Do you need a new dress for the occasion or something?" Diana had always made a fuss about not having a thing to wear.

"Of course not," Sara said quickly. Did he think she was hinting he buy her more clothes? "I'm just not sure I'll fit in with your friends. I don't want to embarrass you. Why don't you go by yourself?"

Jason shook his head. "I hired you as my fiancée. Now the only way to give the situation credibility is for you to act like one. You did great with Dee-dee, so I don't see what the problem is here. Just think of it as another acting lesson, or whatever."

Her face flamed at the memory of the kiss they'd exchanged. Were they going to have to act the part of a couple madly in love in front of his friends?

Jason didn't want her to think he was deliberately embarrassing her by referring to the day Dee-dee had visited Kelsey. "This is important, Sara. If necessary, the Wiltons will testify on our behalf that we are engaged, but I don't want my friends to have to lie for me."

"But all this is a lie."

"Only if you want to quit," Jason said. "My offer of marriage is still open."

Sara turned her face to the fire. She had no intention of accepting Jason's offer. Marriage was a bond between two people who loved each other.

"I'll come to the Wiltons' with you a week after the Bintys have been here," she said quietly. "That should give Kelsey time to adjust."

"Fair enough." Jason tried convincing himself the relief and happiness he felt at her agreement was normal. Having her meet his friends was, after all, a part of the charade. He didn't have much success, however. He was already looking forward to a dinner engagement that wasn't even set up yet.

"It's very, very strange, Father," Mrs. Binty said as she rinsed a plate.

"What is?" Binty looked up from the dish he was drying.

"Himself and Miss Sara, that's what."

Mr. Binty sighed. They'd arrived here Sunday night. It was Tuesday morning. He knew from past experience that that was long enough for the snap judgments his wife made of people.

"It's not our business," he tried to remind her, though the statement had never had any effect on her.

"They act very cool for an engaged couple. No hugs or kisses, no time alone without the little one, and none of that other stuff we see on the telly, either."

"Now, Mother, that's none of our business. They're both nice."

"That they are," Mrs. Binty agreed. "It's a relief to know they're nothing like that terrible couple we worked for last summer. Sara asked me to tell you she wants us both to stop calling her 'miss.' She and the little one are real easy to take care of. I don't know much about Himself yet."

It was a relief to know she was off the subject. "Where's Miss Sara now?"

"Reading the book she bought yesterday. It took some persuading to get her to go downstairs and look around the shops while the little one napped."

"She's kind of shy, isn't she?" Mr. Binty said.

"That she is. Know what she got?"

"No."

"A book on etiquette. The serious way she's reading it, is strange. Makes me wonder if she's afraid of displeasing him."

"Why would she be afraid?" Binty asked in exasperation.

"That's what I'd like to know."

Sara's new routine surprised Jason. He knew she'd been to the stores downstairs because Mrs. Binty had mentioned it, but other than that she'd done nothing else.

What on earth could she possibly find to do in her room? There was no television set in there and when he went past her door, she didn't even have the radio on.

The Bintys were a wonderful couple and Kelsey had taken to them quicker than she'd made friends with anyone except Sara. There was no need for Sara to stick around the apartment, but she did.

Jason wanted to know what had made her the way she was. It was close to three weeks since they'd met and he barely knew her. Her smiles and laughs were for Kelsey. With him, she was reserved and quiet. It was four days since the Bintys had come. Four days in which the only words Sara had said to him were "good morning" and "good night."

It was time he had a talk with her. He had to tell her they were dining with Peter and Meera Wilton on Saturday, which wouldn't be difficult. He also had to bring up the subject of what she would wear to the dinner, which from past experience he knew *would* be difficult. Very difficult.

Jason came home on Thursday for lunch and, on impulse, mentioned he'd decided to take the afternoon off.

"It's a fine day for a walk in the park, or shopping," Mrs. Binty suggested as she served them tomato soup and roast beef sandwiches. "Kelsey's going down for her nap, and then Mr. Binty and I are going to take her to feed the ducks."

It would give him the chance to talk to Sara. "Would you like to come for a walk with me, Sara?"

She looked surprised. Lifting the napkin from her lap she wiped her mouth. "For a walk?"

You'd think he'd suggested they go skinny-dipping in the Thames in the middle of the day. "Yes."

Color shot into her face. She looked around the kitchen as if she wanted a bolt hole. Her gaze flicked from Mrs. Binty, who stood by the table taking a personal interest in the conversation, to him.

"A walk in the park will get the color in your cheeks. I won't have it said as how you came to England, and grew plain and thin," Mrs. Binty said.

"I'm just naturally pale." Sara looked at Jason. "Couldn't we wait till Kelsey's awake, and then all three of us go to the park?"

Half a loaf was better than nothing. "All right. Call me when she's up and ready. I've got a few things to do till then."

Sara felt a light breeze stir her hair as they walked across the park. It was a beautiful day, and she loved the feel of the sun on her face and arms. Kelsey held on to both their hands till they got to the pond in the park. Sara sat down close to the water with Kelsey beside her. The greedy, pampered ducks sensed a food line and swam up to them.

"The Wiltons suggested Saturday night for the dinner, if that's all right with you."

Jason liked the way the afternoon sun filtered through the weeping willow, casting a pattern of light and shade on Sara's delicate face.

"That's fine."

Sara bit her lip nervously. Was there a patron saint of eating out who would watch over her so that she used the right fork every time and committed no other social blunders?

"Penny for them?"

"Excuse me?" She turned her face to Jason, who'd sat down on a bench three feet away.

"I'm willing to pay a penny for your thoughts."

"They're not worth that." She stood and wiped her hands down the sides of her pants. "I was just thinking of Claire."

Jason's brows snapped together. "Are you homesick?"

"Not really. I just miss some things."

Here it comes, he thought. The long list of complaints. Diana had been chock-full of them.

"Like?"

"Like nachos smothered in cheese sauce and jalapeños, being able to drive myself places and...."

"You want a car of your own?"

She looked surprised. "Of course not. What would I do with a car here? I don't know how to drive on the wrong side of the road. It's just that at home I took it for granted that I could go anywhere, any time I wanted. Here, it seems like going out needs so much planning, I don't want to do it. I don't like the feeling that my own fears might keep me inside."

"It's only because it's all so new for you. Let me see if I can come up with an idea that might help."

She looked startled. "It's not your problem. I wasn't complaining. I'm really happy here. You've given me so much, and I feel I haven't done anything to earn the salary you pay me."

Her distress sounded loud and clear. "I know you're not complaining, Sara, but a good salary hardly insures happiness."

"It does for me. I'm fine, really I am."

Jason stood and went to sit beside Sara and Kelsey. Why did the money he was paying her represent so much to her?

Taking the bread his daughter handed him, he broke it into pieces and threw it to the ducks. Carefully neutral, he began by saying, "Sara, did your uncle pay you for all you did for him?"

The color drained from her face. "He gave my mother and I a roof over our heads and food to eat and clothes to wear."

"Did he love you?"

Sara looked at him. "My mother loved me," was all she said.

"I asked about your uncle, Sara."

A wisp of hair blew against her trembling lips. "Uncle Samuel didn't love anybody."

The words came out loaded with the pain of emptiness. Jason got to his feet. This wasn't the time to pursue the topic.

Sara stared at a troop of yellow ducklings. Had she sounded whiny? Jason was always catching her at unguarded moments. She stole a glance at him. He'd become very quiet. Was he thinking about Kelsey and the custody case again? She saw the worry creep into his eyes sometimes as he looked at his daughter. If only there was something more she could do to help him.

Kelsey tugged at her arm, and Sara held Kelsey's hand, taking her closer to the edge so the three-year-old could dip her fingers into the water.

Jason watched them. He trusted Sara with Kelsey in a way he hadn't trusted anyone ever before. Quiet, unassuming, without even trying, she'd made more of an impression on him than any woman he'd met. She'd used the word "ordinary" in describing herself once. He wished the world held more ordinary people like Sara. People who believed in absolute integrity, who didn't say one thing and mean another, who did their best because it was their way, not because they had to. Sara had given ordinary a whole new meaning. There had to be something he could do for her...something special.

Sara looked up and their gazes tangled. For a minute there was a new message in her eyes...the kind of message a woman sent a man when their relationship edged out of the area of just knowing each other into a new field.

I like you.

Jason tensed. Had the thought really arced between them, or was the fresh air and sunshine affecting his imagination?

"It's time we were getting back."

Nothing in Sara's voice as she stood and brushed the crumbs from her pants indicated anything unusual had happened. Jason reached for Kelsey, who was holding her arms up. He hadn't gotten around to the second thing he'd wanted to tell Sara.

The box was waiting at the flat when they got back.

"There's something here for you," Mrs. Binty announced, putting the black and gold box in Sara's hands.

"For me?" Sara stared at the name Rudolfo's on the cover. Hadn't she seen that name somewhere recently?

"Open it."

Sara did, wondering what was going on. Her hands shook as she moved the tissue paper and picked up the purple outfit. The pants were silk, the short jacket covered with sequins.

"Do you like it?"

Sara spun around. Jason was leaning against the door.

"It's for the dinner with the Wiltons. Do you like it?"

Sara opened her mouth, then closed it. It was all part of the job...only a dummy would have to be told over and over again. The warm feeling that she'd carried back with her melted away. Jason was spending a great deal of money on her. She had to make sure she didn't mess up.

Aware that Mrs. Binty was staring at her curiously, Sara said, "It's very pretty. Thank you, Jason."

Enough enthusiasm to fill an eggcup. Great. Swallowing disappointment and frustration, he said mildly, "If it doesn't fit, the store will be happy to alter it for you."

"Thank you." Sara's voice sounded too polite. "If you'll excuse me, I'd better go and try it on."

Jason was left staring at the empty box. You'd think he'd given her a hair shirt.

Sara stared at herself in the mirror in her bedroom. She'd never worn anything so beautiful. The pants were attached to a bustier-type top. The jacket, left open, made her neck look long and elegant. Sara gathered up her hair and held it on top of her head. The deep purple added color to her face, making her look almost pretty.

If only she didn't have so many freckles. If only she was less plain.

Briskly, Sara took off the outfit, donning her regular clothes. Wishing for the moon would get her nowhere. Freckles or no freckles, it didn't make a difference. Jason was her boss and that was that.

Chapter Five

The Wiltons surprised Sara. About Jason's age, there was nothing critical or condescending about them as there had been with Dee-dee. Meera Wilton's parents had come out to England from India when she was three. Peter and she had met at Cambridge. They'd been married six years, had a little boy the same age as Kelsey, and were expecting their second child.

By the time their drinks were served, Sara had decided she liked the warm, talkative Meera.

Hearing she hadn't done any sight-seeing so far, Meera said, "I would love to show you around London."

"I'm not sure—" Sara began hesitantly when Jason cut in.

"She'd love that. I was just considering hiring a guide for her. Someone who would make it fun and interesting."

Sara blinked. Why would Jason want to make things fun and interesting for her?

"Aren't you going to take her around yourself?" Peter asked.

Jason shook his head. "I can't for the next few days and I don't want her to feel tied to the apartment. Meera, if you're sure?"

"I'd love to." She smiled at Sara. "I haven't been doing too much lately because of this pregnancy, but now I'm over the morning sickness, I want to enjoy myself till it's show-time."

"I don't want to bother you," Sara protested. "You've got a little boy and you must need to rest."

"We've got a really good nanny for Sean, and he goes to a private nursery school for half a day, anyway. As for resting, pregnancy's a condition, not an illness."

"How is Sean doing?" Sara stole a look at Jason's face. There had been a note in his voice that got there when he was upset about something.

"He's fine," Peter said. "Has so many friends. Came home yesterday and told Meera that he had asked someone to marry him."

Though Jason smiled, Sara sensed what he was feeling immediately. Sean's accomplishments reminded him of Kelsey's handicap. She looked at Meera, who was glaring at her husband. Sara reached under the table for Jason's hand.

"Kelsey worked out a twenty-five piece puzzle in no time yesterday," she said quickly. "When I worked in a pre-school, I knew three- and four-year-olds who couldn't put a twelve-piece together. I play a math game with her, and she can match up numbers and symbols right away, up to ten."

Meera guessed what she was trying to do. "Sean's slow about things like that," she said. "Must take after Peter's side of the family."

The joke lightened the atmosphere. Jason had never been so surprised in all his life as when Sara had gripped his hand.

The fact she'd guessed his pain, that she'd reached out to comfort him, had eased some of the tightness around his chest. Some of his close friends knew how he worried over Kelsey, but no one had ever done what Sara had...sensed his pain and shared in it. And no one had defended Kelsey as if she were her own cub.

He looked at her, aware that her gaze searched his face for signs of stress. Finding none, she made to withdraw her hand, but Jason turned his so that his fingers linked through Sara's and let their clasped hands rest on his thigh under the table.

Jason glanced at Sara a little later as she talked with Meera. She'd done her hair in some kind of braid that drew attention to her slender neck and the delicate bones of her face. Purple was a good color on her.

He was glad he'd insisted on the dinner with the Wiltons. Meera and Peter, with their easygoing manner, had put Sara at ease. He knew his friends liked Sara, too, or Meera would never have offered to take her around. The Wiltons had met Diana once, and no one had suggested a repeat, but now Meera couldn't stop talking about the places she wanted to show Sara. When the women had gone to the rest room, Peter had clapped him on the back and said, "Found the treasure trove finally, did you, old chap? Sara's a wonderful woman."

All three of them laughed now at something Peter had said. Aware they were looking at him, Jason smiled. He'd better pay attention to the conversation.

In the car going home, Sara turned to Jason. "I really don't have all that much time to go around with Meera. Maybe I can call her and tell her so."

"No. I want you to take her up on her invitation. Kelsey's doing great with the Bintys, so there's nothing for you to do at the apartment anyway."

Sara said nothing, but for a few minutes Jason had reminded her of Uncle Samuel. Firm, unbending, domineering. The change in him was so sudden it frightened her. Had his warm, friendly manner this evening been just an act for the Wiltons?

Sara leaned back in her seat, feeling very tired. She'd enjoyed the evening, but it was time to get back to reality now.

Three weeks to the day he had met Sara, Jason put his key into the lock and turned it. His daughter's laugh reached his ears, bringing a smile to his lips. It was a sound he was definitely getting used to. Setting the briefcase down, he hurried toward them.

Sara was in Kelsey's bedroom, playing a simple game of peek-a-boo. Kelsey saw him and flung herself at him. Jason felt the familiar rush of love as he hugged his daughter.

Please let Kelsey start talking soon. Please let there be nothing wrong with her, he prayed silently as he kissed the top of her silky head.

His gaze met Sara's over his daughter. She wore her usual skirt and sweater. He'd asked Meera to take her shopping, but Meera had reported through Peter that Sara had refused to buy anything.

"Did you have a good day?"

Some kind of charge passed between them, and Sara got to her feet, unaccountably nervous. How was it, after a long day at work, he still managed to look so good? "Yes, thank you. Excuse me. I'm going to start dinner."

Jason frowned at the old familiar refrain. He'd thought all that was behind them. "Where are the Bintys?"

"I—I gave them the afternoon off. One of their granddaughters had her tonsils removed this morning in Woolich, and they were anxious to see her. They'll be back in the morning."

She looked at him as if she expected him to open his mouth and roar fire at her like the dragon in one of Kelsey's books.

"That's fine with me," he said mildly, watching Sara relax. Had she been worried that he would be upset by her decision? "I have a better idea. You give Kelsey her bath, and I'll fix dinner."

Sara's eyes widened. Bathing Kelsey was one of Jason's favorite tasks. She had never seen him happier than when he came out of the bathroom, his shirt and pants soaked, his towel-wrapped little girl in his arms.

"Are you sure?" she asked, taking Kelsey from him and balancing her on her hip.

She watched him drag his tie off, undo the top button of his shirt, and begin to roll up his shirtsleeves.

"I'm sure. What with the Bintys and you taking over all the cooking, I haven't done any in a while."

Sara flushed. Did Jason resent the fact that he'd lost all his privacy by this new arrangement?

Jason stared at her as she walked out with Kelsey. Now what had he said to make her look as if he'd just stepped on her? The woman was an unsolvable mystery.

Forty-five minutes later Sara stepped out of the bathroom and took a deep breath. Kelsey immediately did the same. Sara smiled as she put Kelsey down and followed the toga-wrapped three-year-old into the child's bedroom.

"That smells good, doesn't it? Let's get you dressed and see what Daddy's made for dinner."

Kelsey ran to the bottom drawer of her chest, opened it and took out the nightie she wanted to wear and clean underwear.

Sara slipped the blue gown over the child's head. Her mind went back to the look she'd seen earlier in Jason's eyes. He was very worried about Kelsey. At least she'd had the experience with the little boy in the preschool to convince her it was only a matter of time before Kelsey started speaking. Jason had nothing to hold on to, except hope.

She stopped abruptly in the doorway of the kitchen. Kelsey had run on ahead and was already seated at the table, her bib around her neck.

"I thought we'd eat in here tonight."

"That's fine."

Mr. Binty insisted on serving the evening meal in the formal dining room. Sara stared at the table. Jason had set the table, even putting a single rose in a vase in the middle of it. Her eyes were held by the packages on the counter. Had he slipped downstairs to the deli to get something for dinner?

"Sit," he said, drawing a chair out with a flourish.

Sara sat. She couldn't see anything on the stove top, so whatever it was Jason had made had to be in the oven.

"I took out the salad Mrs. Binty left in case you don't like what I've made."

He opened the oven door as Sara watched. Her eyes widened as he took out a huge baking tray.

"Nachos?" she asked, a note of disbelief in her voice.

"Smothered in cheese sauce." Jason set the tray down and produced a can from the refrigerator. "And jalapeños."

The tears came so quick, she had no time to think up an excuse.

"Hey!" Jason said, looking at her face. "What's wrong?"

"Nothing." Sara shook her head and grabbed at a paper napkin from the holder in the center of the table.

Kelsey's face crumpled and she leaned toward Sara. Jason picked his daughter up, but she didn't want to stay with him. He put her on Sara's lap and looked at both of them in exasperation.

"You said you liked them," he reminded Sara, his heart sinking. "You didn't say they made you cry."

"Oh, Jason." Sara laughed and looked at Kelsey, who was looking very worried. "It's all right, sweetheart. I'm not really crying. Daddy just surprised me, that's all."

Unconvinced, Kelsey put her arms around Sara and laid her head against her chest. Sara reached for a nacho, and looked at Jason. Was he annoyed by her reaction? "Thank you for going to all this trouble, Jason."

"When was the last time someone did something for you, Sara?"

Her mouth quivered, and he said quickly, "Don't answer that. Just prove you like them by eating them all up."

Sara reached for a nacho, then another. As her taste buds responded, she couldn't help the long "Mmm-hmm" of appreciation that left her mouth. The bland corn chips, the tangy cheese sauce and the bite of the jalapeños provided a wonderful complement of tastes.

Jason smiled. "You do like them," he said, heaping some more on the plate in front of her.

Kelsey decided life was back to normal and turned around on Sara's lap. Picking up a nacho, she bit into it.

"Mmm-hmm."

The sound was an exact reproduction of the one Sara had made. Both adults froze. Except for laughs and sneezes and coughs, this was the first sound they'd heard Kelsey imitate.

Jason gripped Sara's hand hard.

"Did you hear that?" He was afraid his longing to hear his daughter speak had conjured up the sound.

"Yes." Sara's heart leapt with excitement as she turned to Kelsey. "You like nachos, don't you, sweetheart? Let's hear you say mmm-hmm again. It's so good."

"Mmm-hmm," Kelsey repeated obligingly.

Sara hoped Kelsey would add "good" or something to the sound, but she just smiled at them.

It was enough for the two adults. Sara looked at her hand. Jason's grip made it feel quite numb, but heat of a different kind shot up her arm and down her spine.

"I'm sorry." Jason released her hand and stared at the imprint of his fingers. "I didn't mean to hurt you. Shall I get you a wet towel to wrap around it?"

"Of course not." Sara reached for another nacho. "There's nothing wrong with my hand."

"I was just so excited..."

"I know. I was, too."

They looked at Kelsey, who had cheese sauce dripping down her chin.

"She'll talk when she's ready," Sara said, glimpsing the yearning in Jason's eyes for reassurance.

"I know."

When Sara got to her feet after the meal was over to gather up the plates, Jason placed his hand on her arm. "I made the mess in here. I'm going to clean up."

"You've done enough. Let me load the dishwasher."

He'd stayed up late last night working and had left early this morning. He must be tired.

"No, Sara."

"Cleaning up is woman's work," she tried again.

"Woman's work?" Jason looked as if she'd hit him over the head with something. "What do you mean?"

"Well...I don't come into your office and do your work, and you're pretty tired tonight. I think you should let me help you with this."

"There's no law that says you have to do it, Sara. After Di died, I moved out of the house in Pasadena, and let the staff go. I took care of Kelsey all by myself for two months." He laughed. "I passed a crash course in Housework 101 with flying colors. Later I got someone to watch her in the daytime, but till I moved to Rainbow Valley and hired Mrs. Garcia, I still fixed the evening meal and cleaned up. There *is* no woman's work, or man's work. It's just whoever feels like doing it.''

Sara watched Jason tie Mrs. Binty's apron on. His words left a warm feeling in her until she realized what he'd said. Her heart sank. He'd taken two months off from his work to mourn his wife? He must have loved her very, very much.

He began to clear the table and, against her will, her gaze followed. Jason's attitude was so different from Uncle Samuel's. Her mother's brother had never picked up after himself or even put the newspaper back together after he'd read it. He'd always taken for granted the fact Sara or her mother would do it.

''I'll read to Kelsey till you come in.''

She didn't want Jason thinking she was usurping another privilege.

''That's fine.''

Kelsey fell asleep after the first story, worn out by the two hours she had spent at the park and her long bath. Sara began to tidy the room. There were a couple of Jason's books on business management on the floor. Kelsey loved carrying her father's books around and pretending to read them.

Sara picked up the first one and it slipped out of her grasp. The second time she picked it up, she saw the corner of a photograph sticking out. Pulling it out, she looked at it, her breath catching in the middle of her chest.

The woman in the picture had to be Jason's wife. She had a glorious mane of red hair, a beautifully made-up face and an exquisite choker of emeralds and diamonds that drew attention to her green eyes.

The hair was like Kelsey's, but the eyes weren't. Sara couldn't tear her gaze away from the picture. Jason's wife had been very sophisticated. The expression in her eyes also said this was a woman who had been very sure of herself. They must have been a very attractive couple.

Sara jumped when she felt the picture being taken out of her hands. She stared at the poker expression on Jason's face. His gaze fixed on his sleeping daughter, he ripped the photograph into shreds. Frozen, Sara could think of nothing to say as he moved forward to kiss Kelsey's cheek and tuck the blanket in around her.

She was still silent as he left the room. Sitting down in the rocking chair, she set it in motion. There was sweat on her forehead and her palms were clammy. Had Jason thought she was prying into his things? That must have been why he'd looked so angry. She couldn't have felt more uneasy if she'd stood on the brink of a volcano and discovered it wasn't dormant.

Jason was still very much in love with his wife. What was it he'd said earlier? He'd moved out of the house he'd shared with her, let the staff go because he hadn't wanted anyone to remind him of the time his wife had been alive. Then there was the way he'd torn Diana's picture up, angry that she'd been looking at it. He had no room in his life for anyone other than Kelsey.

Sara had a hard time falling asleep that night. Why had Jason fixed the nachos for her? It wouldn't do to attach any importance to it, he'd simply remembered what she'd said about missing them. Under all his impatience, Jason was kind and generous.

Maybe, Sara thought as sleep finally claimed her, not all men were alike.

Jason stared out the window of his room. The darkness outside matched his memories of Di. He'd thought he'd gotten rid of all the pictures, but one must have been left in that old book on Sara's lap.

The sight of Di's smiling face reminded him of how he had failed her as a husband. Why hadn't he guessed she hadn't been ready to be a mother? That she would never be? Women like Di were never meant to be mothers, but at that time he'd thought the baby would change Di, that she'd settle down. He'd been so wrong. Kelsey's birth and Di's attitude to the child had been the final straw in their relationship. Di had started partying and drinking heavily with a crowd of like-minded people. On the night she'd been killed, she'd left a club in Los Angeles with another man. The man had been a political bigwig and he'd pulled strings to see that his name was kept out of it. Jason couldn't have cared less—the man had just been one of many. Even Dee-dee didn't know about the other man or that Diana had been seeing him. Jason hadn't wanted to disillusion her completely; it had been hard enough for Dee-dee to lose her only child.

The demons of the past had chased him for too long. To keep them at bay, Jason went to his computer. When he looked up from his work, it was 3:00 a.m. Removing the glasses he wore when he worked, he pinched the bridge of his nose.

A sound brought him to his feet automatically. His mind on Kelsey, Jason headed for her room. He stopped in the doorway. The soft light of the lamp on the dresser showed Sara in the rocking chair, Kelsey in her arms. She was crooning a soft melody, keeping the rocker in motion with her foot.

Jason leaned against the door, absorbing the scene, letting it wash out some of the earlier bitterness. It didn't surprise him that Sara had gotten here before he had.

Sara shifted in the chair and he went to her. "Let me take her. She's getting heavy."

She shook her head. "You'll only wake her again."

"Is she sick?"

"No. It's just a bad dream. I'm going to put her back to bed soon."

Unwilling to leave, Jason sat down on the carpet, leaning against the chest of drawers. Tilting his head back, he closed his eyes for a minute.

Sara looked at him, glad the soft lamplight hid the fact she was staring. She'd seen the light in his room, knew he hadn't gone to bed. Had memories of his wife kept him awake, or had she upset him so much that he couldn't sleep?

"I—I didn't mean to pry earlier. I was just picking up the books Kelsey had brought in here and the photograph fell out."

Jason opened his eyes. "I know you weren't prying. You're not the type."

"She was very beautiful. Kelsey looks like her."

"And I hope the resemblance will end there." The harshness in Jason's voice surprised Sara. "Beauty that's skin deep doesn't impress me. I want Kelsey to be beautiful inside."

Jason's words startled Sara. He didn't sound like a man in love with a memory.

"I don't want Kelsey growing up headstrong and spoiled," he added.

The words made something inside Sara shrink. Had Jason and his wife not gotten along because Kelsey's mother had had a mind of her own?

Uncle Samuel had called her that when she'd told him about the job she'd gotten at the day care. *Headstrong*. Like Uncle Samuel, did Jason feel women shouldn't have opinions, or make their own decisions? That they should be ruled by the men in the household?

Kelsey stirred in her arms, and Sara told herself she had no business criticizing her boss. It was time she went back to her own room. Getting to her feet, she winced.

Jason was beside her in a minute. "What is it?"

"It's my right foot. It's fallen asleep." It had a tendency to cramp up when she sat a certain way. Sara leaned most of her weight on her left foot, waiting for sensation to return to the other one. The pins and needles were so bad she bit her lip.

"Here, let me take Kelsey."

As Jason took his daughter, the back of his hand brushed against Sara's breast. When she'd heard Kelsey cry she hadn't stopped for a robe. Jason's touch burned through the thin lawn of her nightgown.

"I'm sorry," he said immediately.

Awkward situations will have to be handled professionally.

She hadn't realized it would get *this* awkward, or that she would react like a teenager who was all hormones and no self-control.

"That's all right."

Why on earth did she have to sound as if she'd just run a mile?

As Jason tucked his daughter in, Sara said a quick goodnight, and limped out of the room.

Jason woke late the next morning, glad it was Saturday and he didn't have to go to work. Maybe he would take Kelsey and Sara for a drive into the country.

Sara. He linked his hands behind his head. No woman had taken up so much of his thoughts as the little golden brown owl did. It wasn't her looks or her body: the things that usually drew him to a woman. With Sara, it was something more elusive, something he couldn't name.

It was the way she smiled at Kelsey, the way the color ran up under her skin when he paid her a compliment, the way she told the Bintys to sit down and rest while she made them a pot of tea. The little things she did tugged at him in a way nothing had in a long time.

He'd never talked about Diana to anyone, yet last night he'd wanted to tell Sara about her, explain why he'd torn Di's picture up. Jason's jaw clenched. He had to keep things with Sara on a strictly business footing.

Jason found Sara and Kelsey coloring in the kitchen, a plate of the cookies Mrs. Binty called biscuits beside them. As Kelsey reached for one, Sara snatched it away, said, "Mine," and popped it into her mouth. Kelsey's giggles filled the kitchen, warming Jason's heart.

The aroma of baking bread filled the kitchen as Mrs. Binty bustled between sink and oven. In a corner Mr. Binty sat reading the paper.

As always, Sara talked to Kelsey as if there was nothing unusual about a one-sided conversation. "That's a wonderful picture, Kelsey. We'll put it up on the refrigerator and when Daddy sees it, he'll know you made it for him. He's going to be so proud of you, and he's going to say, 'Thank you, Kelsey, for making me such a great picture.'"

"Thank you, Kelsey, for making me such a great picture."

His words changed the scene in front of him. Sara looked at him and blushed bright red. Kelsey ran to him. Mr. Binty jumped up and said, "I'll get your coffee, sir," and Mrs. Binty immediately said something about scrambled eggs and bacon.

"I'll only have coffee now, thank you." Jason took the third small chair, and kissed the top of his daughter's head. "Good morning, sweetheart."

Why was Sara twisting the paper off a crayon and refusing to look at him? Was she still embarrassed about the way his hand had touched her last night?

"I'm going jogging in the park, but when I come back, would you and Kelsey like to drive out to the country? We could take a picnic."

"It's ever such a nice day for a picnic," Mrs. Binty said while Sara just stared at Jason as if he'd suggested she should grow two horns on the top of her head.

"If I might make a suggestion, sir, the downs are particularly beautiful now." Mr. Binty handed Jason a mug of coffee.

"Thank you. We might go there. Sara?"

"That's fine with me, but if you'd rather go alone with Kelsey, I have plenty of things to do h-here."

Aware of the looks of surprise on the Bintys' faces, Jason said, "We want you to come with us, don't we, Kelsey? What's a picnic without a fiancée?"

Sara's eyes widened at the reminder of her role. On impulse, Jason leaned over and kissed her full on the lips. Her mouth quivered under his. Her dazed look heated his blood, but he forced himself to get to his feet. "Well, that's settled. Shall we leave at eleven?"

"It'll do you all good to get some roses in your cheeks," Mrs. Binty said after Jason had left the room. "And I'll have a nice picnic lunch ready for you to take. A young couple need to spend time together. You and Himself are having problems, aren't you, dearie?"

Sara stared at Mrs. Binty blankly. She liked the plump, cheerful Englishwoman and her tall, gaunt husband.

Looking into Mrs. Binty's warm brown eyes, she realized not much got past the intelligent woman.

"A f-few." It was better she thought that, than guess the truth. "Jason's very busy with his work right now."

"All the more reason to spend a day away from it. And if you'd like a word of advice, these days a woman doesn't wait for a man to make the first move. My daughters didn't. Some men have starting trouble, if you catch my meaning."

Sara nodded acknowledgment of Mrs. Binty's advice before she left the kitchen. Amid the confusing swirl of excitement and anxiety of spending more time with Jason was one clear thought. If Jason wanted the Bintys to testify on his behalf, as well, they'd have to do a better job of convincing the perceptive couple that they were madly in love.

Chapter Six

"I thought we'd take the M40 out of London and then head west to an area called Burnham Beeches," Jason said as he drove out of London. "It isn't too far away from here and I'm not too sure how Kelsey's going to take a longer drive. If I remember correctly, Burnham Beeches is very pretty, with lots of different trees. Do you think you might like that?"

"Anything's fine with me."

Sara wasn't used to the way Jason always asked her opinion, so she gave it automatically.

"If you'd like to look at the map, you can see how we're heading for Cookham in the Thames valley. Burnham Beeches is east of Cookham."

Sara opened the map and studied it. England was chock-full of interesting places to see.

Silence filled the car as Kelsey fell asleep in her car seat. Sara stared out the window, spellbound by the English countryside. It was exactly as the English poets she loved to read described it. Fields of wildflowers, thatched cottages, quaint villages and the occasional pub.

"Are you hungry, or thirsty?" Jason asked after a while.

"Don't stop for me. I could keep going. It's all so beautiful." Sara leaned back in her seat.

From the books he'd seen around the apartment he knew Sara's taste in reading leaned toward poetry, essays and human interest stories. Mrs. Binty had mentioned that Sara had asked her how to get to the nearest library.

"As soon as I can take a day off, we'll leave Kelsey with the Bintys and visit Stratford-upon-Avon."

Sara's breath caught in her throat at the thought of a whole day alone with Jason. It took a minute longer for her to realize that thought had come first—before the one that visiting Shakespeare's birthplace had been a dream she'd never thought would ever come true.

She glanced at Jason's profile. Why was he being so kind to her? Was it to ensure that she gave her best to Kelsey? A glance over her shoulder showed the little girl fast asleep. Sara's gaze softened. Jason didn't have to worry that she'd be anything but nice to Kelsey.

"I'm going to keep on driving. That way Kelsey will get her nap in and we can get deeper into the country."

"Sounds fine to me," Sara said, turning her gaze back to the rolling fields of knee-high grass and wildflowers.

"How do you like what you've seen of London so far?"

Meera and she had gone out three times. "I loved Westminster Abbey, the bookstores in Charing Cross Road and Portobello Market. Going around with Meera gives me an insider's viewpoint of London. She's full of stories."

Sara bit her lip. She had almost said that the sights and sounds of London had given her grist for the writing mill. She'd had to keep the correspondence classes she'd taken at eighteen a secret from Uncle Samuel. Having her lessons mailed to Claire's address, she'd worked on them after Uncle Samuel had gone to bed. No one other than her friend knew that Sara liked to write essays that were humorous observations on life. Since coming to London, she wrote early each morning, before Kelsey got up.

"Some of the bookstores have readings by famous authors. You might like to go to them."

"Yes." She remembered his having mentioned it before, but now she wondered if Jason's instinctive understanding of what she needed was because he'd had so much practice with his daughter. It couldn't be anything else.

The spot they finally stopped at made Sara wish she could paint. The scene in front of her eyes was meant to be captured for posterity. A huge oak, fifty yards away from the road, provided the perfect place for their picnic. In the distance, sheep and cows grazed, and somewhere she could hear a stream gurgling softly. The soft grass was dotted with flowers of every color.

While Jason got Kelsey out of her car seat, Sara walked ahead with the picnic basket and the red-and-white blanket Mrs. Binty had given her. Spreading it out, she watched as Jason lay a still sleepy Kelsey on the blanket.

"I'll stay with her if you'd like to go for a walk."

"Not right now." Sara knelt in front of the basket and opened it. "Would you like something to drink?"

"Please."

She poured some iced lemonade into three glasses and held Kelsey's for her while she took a long drink.

"You had a nice nap, didn't you, sweetheart?" she said. "Let's have lunch and then we'll go for a small walk and get some pretty flowers. See the cows? You know what the cows say, don't you? Moo. And the sheep? Baa-aa."

Returning from the car with two folding chairs, Jason caught the last of Sara's words. "Know what daddies say?"

he asked, a smile on his face. "Daddies say, 'I'm hu-u-ungry.'"

At his roar, Sara's laughter mingled with Kelsey's giggles. The sound drew Jason and his gaze rested on her mouth. Had anyone told Sara what a sweet laugh she had?

Sara froze. Why on earth was Jason looking at her mouth like that? A wave of heat swept through her as she put a finger up to her lower lip. Did she have something stuck there?

The gesture reminded Jason that he was staring. He turned away to set up the chairs. What on earth was the matter with him?

Sara opened the wicker basket that had been designed by a genius who had found a spot for everything they might need. Taking out the plates, she set them on the blanket and then put out the food. Mrs. Binty had put in deviled eggs and three different kinds of sandwiches—roast beef, cold chicken and mayonnaise, and Sara's favorite, thin slices of cucumber with a little bit of butter. There were cookies, plum cake and homemade English toffee to go with it.

"Is this some kind of a message that we shouldn't hurry back?" Jason asked as he noticed the quantity of food Mrs. Binty had packed.

She laughed. "I think Mrs. Binty is hoping our appetites will improve out in the open."

As they ate, the serenity of their surroundings washed over Sara. It was nice to be here, sense the warmth and love Kelsey and her father shared, be part of their circle for a brief while. She stopped, deviled egg in hand, as a twinge of pain shot through her. This was only a temporary situation.

"Penny for them?" Jason asked, reaching for his fourth sandwich. Why on earth was Sara looking as if someone had punched her in the stomach?

"They aren't worth a penny." Sara mentally shook herself and turned to Kelsey, handing her half a cold chicken sandwich.

He had learned with Sara it was best not to pursue certain subjects. The golden brown owl had stubborn feathers.

"It's so peaceful out here," Sara murmured.

"The country's fine on a day like this," Jason said, "but I don't think you'd like to live here."

"Why not?"

"There's nothing to do."

A few years ago a friend had invited him to use his guest house in the country. He remembered Diana whining nonstop about boredom the entire weekend.

"Nothing to do?" Sara said. "If you had your own garden, Kelsey could run and play outside most of the day, and . . ."

Her voice trailed away. It sounded as if she were discontented with Jason's choice of London as a base. Remembering how he had reacted to his mother-in-law's criticism, Sara held her breath.

"Are you saying you prefer the country to London?"

"It's certainly better than London is for Kelsey."

Jason shook his head impatiently. "Forget Kelsey for a minute. What would *you* do down here?"

"Take long walks, garden, read." And write.

"Peter Wilton's just bought a house in the country. We could visit him and Meera one weekend. That would give you a taste of what it's like to live here."

His tone indicated he didn't think she would like it once she'd tried it on a day-to-day basis. "I don't usually say I'd like something if I don't mean it," Sara said stiffly.

Jason looked at her, eyes narrowed. "You told me you've lived all your life in Rainbow Valley. Granted it's a quiet, peaceful suburb of Los Angeles, but you're just a stone's throw away from any kind of entertainment you could imagine."

"Being a stone's throw away didn't mean I went to all those places."

"Because of your uncle's health?"

"Partly." Uncle Samuel had made more rules than there were days in the year, and the painful lectures even when she went to Claire's place had been hard to take.

The look on Sara's face prompted Jason to say, "What did you do for fun?"

"I read."

Jason's eyes narrowed. He was getting a strange feeling in his gut about Sara's past. "Was your uncle very strict?"

Instead of saying anything, she picked up her glass and drained the lemonade in it. "Sara?"

The contract still bound her to be perfectly honest, but she didn't have to be specific. "Yes, he was." Sara stood and brushed the crumbs off her jeans. "Want to go for a walk, Kelsey?"

Kelsey abandoned the plastic puzzle she had been working on and got to her feet. Watching them leave, Jason realized he had trespassed in an area of Sara's personal life where he really had no business. She wasn't going to tell him any more, but he had plenty of pieces to put together now. The condition of her clothes, her lack of self-esteem, her feeling that she should do all the work.

Jason's eyes narrowed in anger. The uncle had done a real number on her.

He reached for another roast beef sandwich. He'd always thought the longer you knew someone, the easier it became to understand them. Sara was the only exception he knew to that rule. Some kind of misguided sense of loyalty had her clamming up whenever he got too close. Trying to milk one of the cows they'd seen in the fields they'd passed would have been easier than trying to get a glimpse of Sara's past.

He was stretched on his back, fast asleep, when they returned. In sleep he'd lost the strain that was always present on his face. For a moment Sara wanted to reach down and touch him. Kelsey tugged at her hand and Sara turned away. She placed a finger on her lips. "Don't wake Daddy. He's tired. Let's sit by the tree and make daisy chains."

Kelsey looked at her father and then placed a finger on her own lips and nodded.

Jason woke to the sound of Sara's voice. "The prince bent down and lifted Sleeping Beauty to kiss her. The bit of poisoned apple stuck in her throat fell out. Slowly she opened her eyes and looked at the prince. He was so handsome. He bent and kissed her and Sleeping Beauty knew she loved him. They got married and lived happily ever after."

Jason looked at them. Sara must have made the circlets of flowers both she and Kelsey wore like crowns. He guessed she'd had to undo her ponytail to keep the flowers on her head, because her hair framed her face. Kelsey looked like a little cherub, her circlet of flowers already crooked. Warmth filled him at the sight of them both. If only he'd remembered the camera.

"You're both so beautiful," Jason said, watching the color flood Sara's face as her gaze tangled with his.

"Doesn't Kelsey look like a princess?" Sara asked quietly.

"I said, you're *both* beautiful," Jason reiterated.

Sara looked away. Jason was startled by the sadness that brushed her face. Didn't she believe him? Obviously not, for her to look the way she did now.

"Does anyone want to kiss the sleeping daddy and wake *him* up?" he asked.

Kelsey giggled and flew into his arms, while Sara poured tea from a thermos into two mugs and handed Kelsey a covered drinking cup filled with milk. Mrs. Binty had packed chocolate éclairs to go with the tea.

"I think we'll have to continue the practice of having afternoon tea when we get back to the States," said Jason, watching Sara bite into an éclair. They were her favorite pastries, and Mrs. Binty made them very often.

Sara told herself to stop being silly and reading more than there was into every word Jason said. He was just being kind when he'd made that remark about her being beautiful, and whenever he said "we" he meant Kelsey and himself. Besides, she really didn't want to be tied to anyone so soon after Uncle Samuel's death. Or did she?

"I meant what I said earlier about you being beautiful," Jason said as Kelsey drank her milk and held the cup to her doll's mouth. "Don't you believe me?"

"I'm not beautiful." Sara held his gaze though the color that ran up under her skin told him he had embarrassed her again.

The note of finality in her voice angered Jason. Something had to be done about Sara's low self-esteem.

"As a man, I see things that your mirror isn't showing you."

Sara looked at him, her eyes growing large.

"You've got eyes a man can both lose and find himself in, a mouth made for kissing, silky hair that would be wonderful to run one's hands through, and a very sexy smile."

"'Sexy,'" Sara repeated as if she'd never said the word aloud before. Jason had a hard time not smiling. She sounded as if it were an insult.

"Very sexy," he repeated. "You could have any man you want."

Why was Jason teasing her? His words had been casual, but there was nothing casual about the way the blood pounded in her ears or the heat pooled in the pit of her stomach.

Before he could say another word, she began to stuff everything back into the picnic basket. Shutting it, Sara got to her feet and hurried to the car as if she were Cinderella and the clock had just chimed twelve.

Jason smiled at Kelsey, who was puzzled by Sara's quick retreat. As she looked at him for an explanation, Jason experienced a strange surge of happiness. "We're just helping Sara wake up and find her real self," he told his daughter, touching her pert little nose. "It's a shame she didn't wait for me to get to the kissing part."

Jason tried to sort things out in his mind on the drive home. The fact that Sara was barely paying him any attention was beginning to bother him. She'd even asked if she could sit in the back with Kelsey on the way home. That way, she'd said, Kelsey wouldn't get too restless on the long drive. Judging from his daughter's laughter, she loved the game they were playing of This Little Piggy, with her toes.

He shouldn't have embarrassed Sara. He wouldn't have said what he had, except for the fact that she did need waking up. Her reaction had surprised him. She'd looked as if she'd never received any compliments. The women he knew would have begun purring, their eyes demanding he keep on in the same vein. Sara had bolted as if he'd made an indecent suggestion.

Male ego told him Sara was unaware of him as anything other than her employer. He'd never been with another woman who was so...so...self-contained. Any time a little bit of emotion escaped, she gathered it back up and locked it away.

She'd made it very clear she wasn't after his money. She wasn't even after his person. What on earth was important to her?

"Sara, what's the most important thing in the world to you?" he asked when the game in the back stopped for a while.

"Personal freedom."

The answer was so unexpected it startled him. She'd given it so quickly, as if it was something that was always on her mind.

"What does personal freedom mean to you?" he asked.

"Not having to live by someone else's rules. Supporting myself financially, making all my own decisions, choosing what I want to do, or not do."

Jason knew suddenly that the little golden brown owl hadn't had much freedom with her uncle. The vehemence in her voice told him that it was something she cared about very greatly. She and Diana were alike in that respect . . . only at one time Di had pretended she'd wanted marriage and all it stood for.

"Do you think marriage interferes with personal freedom?" he asked Sara.

"Yes. Even living with someone places constraints on that freedom."

"So to achieve what you want, you would have to live alone?"

"Yes."

"Is that what you plan when this job is over?"

"Yes. It's one of the reasons I took it. The money's going to help me support myself till I can find another job."

He had to give her a raise.

"What was it your uncle did before he retired?" he asked Sara.

"He worked in a brokerage house."

The man must have made good money, but he'd obviously had a hard time sharing any of it.

"Did you say he was your mother's brother?"

"Yes."

"Were they very close?"

"No. He was fifteen years old when she was born. He was just like my grandfather, strict and unbending. When my mother met my father, and then he died, my uncle took her in but never let her forget the wrong she had done by letting Cole Adams love her. My mother paid the rest of her life for having me."

"Moses said your uncle was very wealthy."

"I don't want any of his money."

He'd never heard Sara sound so fierce. He looked in the rearview mirror. Kelsey was turning the pages of a book in her car seat, and Sara looked as if she'd answered a call to go to war.

Jason turned on the radio. There was a time to talk and a time to let music cover up the awkwardness. This was definitely time for the latter.

What on earth was he asking so many questions for all of a sudden? Nervous, Sara reached for Kelsey's little foot. "Ready for more of This Little Piggy?" she asked.

That about summed it all up in an acorn shell, Jason thought grimly. Sara Adams preferred playing This Little Piggy, for the fiftieth time, to talking with him. A man would have to be really stupid not to receive the message she was sending.

Let's keep this on a business footing.

Which suited him fine. Just fine. She wasn't his type, anyway.

Thinking back on the day as he sat on the balcony outside his room that night, Jason didn't know what made him angrier. Sara's lack of belief in what he'd said about her looks, or her total lack of interest in him.

He didn't know why the latter irked. He had wanted someone who could be trusted to keep matters on a business footing, someone who wouldn't expect anything from him in the emotional department.

He didn't want any complications in his life, but that didn't mean he shouldn't do something about Sara's lack of confidence in herself as a woman.

Sara leaned back in the tub and hoped the steaming, rose-scented water would ease some of the confusion out of her system. She'd been feeling very unsettled all day... as if all her nerve endings were linked to a cord that Jason controlled.

He was Kelsey's father, her employer, and her pseudo fiancé. Nothing more. Besides, she wanted freedom, not being tied by emotion to any place or person. As soon as Jason was granted custody of Kelsey, he wasn't going to need her anymore.

She had to make her plans for when she would be alone and free at last to explore the freedom she'd always wanted. She'd be able to do exactly as she pleased for a week or two before she'd have to look for another job.

Sara closed her eyes and slid a little deeper into the water. A part of her mind seemed to be backing away from the thought of being all alone. It was only, Sara told herself fiercely, because she'd grown very fond of Kelsey.

Jason looked like a thundercloud when he came to the breakfast table the next morning.

"What's wrong?" Sara asked as soon as Mrs. Binty had taken Kelsey into the playroom. She couldn't possibly ignore the fact that Jason had barely eaten his breakfast. The lines on his face looked as if they had deepened in the last twenty-four hours.

"It's Dee-dee. She'll be here Wednesday."

"Oh."

"I suppose she can't wait to start gathering more evidence to use against me."

"Maybe she'll be different this time," Sara suggested.

She was under no illusion that the woman liked her, but she had caught a glimpse of the way Dee-dee had looked at Kelsey. She loved her granddaughter.

"Dee-dee doesn't know how to be different," Jason snapped. "I'm going to call Moses and tell him to let her know I do not want any surprise visits."

Remembering Dee-dee's last one, Sara felt inclined to agree with Jason, but siding with him against Kelsey's grandmother wouldn't improve matters.

Sara placed a hand on his arm. "I've got an idea. Maybe if Dee-dee stays here, and sees you and Kelsey together, she'll realize how—"

Jason moved away from her, shoved both hands into the pockets of his pants and glared at her. "There's no way I will allow Dee-dee to stay here. You have no idea what you're talking about."

Sara went white. The words had been Uncle Samuel's final remark for everything. "I only thought—"

Jason interrupted her again. "What did you think, Sara? That life is like the fairy tales you read Kelsey and everything will end with 'happily ever after'? Real life is a slap in the face sometimes, but how would you know that? This is the first real problem you've encountered and it isn't even yours, so stay out of it, will you?"

It was a while before Sara realized she was all alone in the room and her mouth was hanging open. Closing it, she picked up her cup of tea with a hand that shook. Wrapping her other hand around it, she held the cup, willing some of the warmth to reach her core.

Her mind buzzed as if her thoughts had turned into a swarm of bees. The stinging kind.

Did you think life is like the fairy tales you read Kelsey and everything will end with "happily ever after"?

This is the first real problem you've encountered....

It isn't even yours, so stay out of it, will you?

The last line went over and over in her head. Jason couldn't have made it clearer she was the hired hand.

As for problems...she thought of Uncle Samuel, and her mother who had worked like a slave and never pleased him. Sara, who had inherited the right to fill Mary Adams's shoes, had suffered because she hadn't been as docile. Coping with his moods had taken all she'd had.

If only Uncle Samuel had shown her a scrap of kindness, life could have been so different. She had lain awake nights, hoping that something would change Uncle Samuel the way people changed in movies and stories. That he would offer love and let them love him in return, but it had never happened.

No, Jason had been wrong when he'd accused her of believing in happy endings.

"Sara?"

She jumped and turned. Jason had changed into sweatpants and a top. "Yes?"

She had wanted to sound casual and cool. The word came out as if she were a frog with laryngitis.

He came into the room. "I didn't mean to yell at you. I'm sorry."

She wasn't sure she had heard right. Jason was apologizing to her?

"It's all right." She'd had plenty of practice at being yelled at. "You're worried about Kelsey and I shouldn't have said anything."

"Yes."

There was an awkward silence and then Jason said, "I'm going for a run."

"It's a nice day for it."

"Would you like to come?"

"Who? Me?" Sara felt the color rise in her face. "No thanks. I have a few things to do."

"See you later, then." Jason seemed about to say something more, but then he turned and left.

"See you later."

As he ran through the park, Jason berated himself with every step that pounded the ground. Why on earth had he taken his temper out on Sara like that? The answer was obvious. He'd been fit to be tied ever since he'd read Dee-dee's letter. He hadn't checked his mail till this morning. The fact that Kelsey was being threatened brought out the worst in him, made him lose all perspective.

Jason pushed his straining muscles to run faster. Sara had looked as if he'd slapped her. His words had wiped out whatever ground he'd gained with her yesterday. Her stilted apology reminded him of their first meeting.

She'd been scared then and she was scared of him now. He'd seen the evidence of tears on her cheeks. He had no business losing control that badly. Just because life had thrown him a curveball, and his marriage had gone sour, was no reason to tell Sara she wasn't entitled to believe in happy endings.

He had to apologize to her all over again, and make it very clear his anger was directed at Dee-dee, not her.

"Where's Sara?" he asked Mrs. Binty the minute he stepped into the kitchen.

"She's gone to church."

"Church?"

His surprise must have shown on his face because Mrs. Binty nodded. "Said she was going for a walk in the park after that, and might not be back till late afternoon."

Her plans must have been made after he'd left. Was she keeping out of the way to give him time to get over his temper completely? A fresh layer of guilt piled onto the heap he already carried. Jason turned away without noticing Kelsey had her hands stretched out to him.

"Well!" said Mrs. Binty, hurrying to the little girl's side. "Never you mind. Your daddy'll be back after he's had his shower. Till then, why don't you and I sit in the rocker, and read that new book Sara bought you."

Kelsey ran to her room and Mrs. Binty followed at a slower pace, content with talking aloud to herself. "If you ask me, I think we've got another story brewing right here under our own roof. I had me suspicions, I did, when she went off looking so sad. And then Himself comes in asking for her and looking so put out to hear she's gone. A nice turn of events, that's what it is, a nice turn of events."

Chapter Seven

Sunday night, Jason worked late at the computer. He planned to stay at the apartment Monday and Tuesday finishing the last-minute things he had to do before a big meeting Wednesday. He also had another plan at the back of his mind.

He woke at nine and the silence told him he might be alone. He should have told Sara what he was planning. After showering, Jason went into the kitchen. The coffee was perking, but there was no sign of anyone.

Pouring himself a mug, he sat down at the kitchen table. A breeze rustled the papers on the table, and Jason grabbed them before they flew away. He was putting them back together when he realized he'd read most of the first page. His interest caught, he turned to the second page.

The sound at the door made him look up. Sara stood there in a long skirt and a sweater, looking terrified.

"Is this yours?" Jason asked, still surprised by the depth of emotion in what he had just read.

She came to the table. "I only write when Kelsey's not here," she said. "Mrs. Binty's taken her to the park, and Mr. Binty's gone to the dry cleaners. I thought you'd left for work."

"This is very good, Sara."

"I just scribble my thoughts down."

"I said, it's good, Sara."

She tried to laugh. "Thank you. It's nothing serious, you know."

"Why do you always put yourself down, Sara?"

"Excuse me?"

"I said, why do you always put yourself down?"

Her hand crept to the neck of her sweater as she stood and looked at him, her heart in her eyes.

"Is it because you want to get there first, do it before anyone else does it to you? Does it hurt less that way?"

"I don't know what you mean."

Jason got to his feet and only six inches of space separated them. "I think you do. Is it your uncle who convinced you you're not worth a damn?"

"Stay out of my personal life, Jason."

"He did it because he was scared of losing you, Sara. Where else could he get an unpaid servant to wait on him hand and foot."

The word *servant* made her flinch as if he'd slapped her, but Jason kept going.

"Your work is good, Sara. Have you shown it to anyone? I know a publisher here—"

Her head came up and her eyes blazed with anger. "Why is it okay for you to tell me what to do, but it isn't okay for me to suggest Dee-dee stay here? Is it because you're a man and men know about what's best for everyone else, or is it because you know how to give advice but can't take any?"

She didn't know who was more surprised by the vehemence of her outburst, Jason or herself. Her heart jumped at the way his eyes narrowed, but she refused to look away. Here it comes, she thought, the anger she'd expected to show up all along. Sara didn't regret saying what was on her mind.

The first prerequisite for freedom was personal courage and she'd had twenty-four years of training for this moment.

Jason turned away and poured himself a cup of coffee as Sara struggled with the impulse to leave the room.

"You know, you're right and I'm wrong." Jason swung around to face her. "I'm sorry. Maybe we should just stay out of each other's personal business."

Sara stared as the kitchen door swung shut behind him. Was it possible to have auditory hallucinations? She was sure Jason had said he was sorry again. Uncle Samuel had never once apologized for a thing. Her mother had said that men's egos made it hard for them to admit they had been in the wrong. Sara thought of Jason as he had stood there, coffee mug in hand. A rush of warmth flooded her. The apology had just sent Jason's stock with her sky-high.

Guilt and worry gripped Jason. Why hadn't she responded to his apology? Was he really being domineering and unfair? Diana had accused him of being high-handed because he had refused to let her get rid of the baby. Sometimes he wondered if she would still have been alive if he'd let her make that decision on her own.

Sara's writing had surprised him with its humor and style. In his eagerness to help her, he'd forgotten that she was a very private person. The very fact that she hadn't mentioned she wrote should have warned him it was something she didn't want to discuss. He thought of the yearning he had glimpsed in her eyes when he'd told her she was good at it.

Why was it so hard for Sara to believe in her own abilities? He thought of the way she was with Kelsey; loving and encouraging, always praising her and telling her how clever she was. Recalling the way she'd sat up with Kelsey when she'd had a bad dream, the way Kelsey turned to Sara instead of to him for her needs these days, Jason knew finding Sara had been the best thing he could have done for his daughter.

Kelsey didn't cling to him the way she used to, neither did she cry when he left in the mornings; she was eating better and her eyes had lost that too solemn expression. Overall, he was happy and relieved at the way Sara and Kelsey got on, though it rankled in a small way that Sara seemed to understand his daughter effortlessly.

He'd read countless books on child psychology, talked to Kelsey's pediatrician almost every week and still he hadn't achieved what Sara had. As for the Bintys...Sara had found a gold mine there. Seeing Kelsey so happy and content freed him to concentrate on his work. His business meetings with prominent car manufacturers here, and in Europe, were going better than he'd expected; the collaborations he was in the process of setting up ensuring greater success than he'd anticipated. Things couldn't have been better.

He owed Sara so much and he was going to do something about it. He'd respect her wishes about her work—he wasn't going to interfere in that aspect of her life—but he was going to do something to remove that veil of low self-esteem that she wrapped herself in.

Sara was reading in the living room three hours later when Jason walked in. She looked up as he muttered something about a briefcase. "It's behind the couch. Kelsey kept running around with it and I thought she might hurt herself, so I hid it.''

"Thank you, Sara." He picked it up and was about to leave the room when he said, "What's that book you're reading?"

"Hardy's *Far from the Madding Crowd*."

"Are you bored?"

"Of course not." Why on earth would anyone be bored with a nice book and time to read it in?

"Oh, by the way..."

"Yes?" Was he going to discuss her work again, tell her she was stubborn not to listen to him?

"Would you mind coming with me to pick out a tie tomorrow? I've got a really important meeting Wednesday and Peter was saying something about my ties being old-fashioned and stuffy."

Sara had noticed. Jason's ties were the kind that had been in fashion ten years ago. So were his suits. She'd just taken it for granted he wasn't interested in clothes.

"I thought you'd help me choose something. You have great taste in clothes. I like the red rompers you bought Kelsey last week."

"I'll come." If Jason could put the argument behind them and extend an olive branch, it was up to her to grasp it. With both hands.

"Thank you. Is eleven all right for you?"

"Eleven's fine."

He nodded and left the room whistling. Something about the whistle made Sara uneasy. What had happened to make Jason so happy all of a sudden?

The sight of the store Jason parked his Jaguar in front of the next day made Sara open her eyes wide. Rudolfo's was a salon with floor-to-ceiling glass windows covered with silk drapes, an intricately painted ceiling, and marble floors. Sara sucked her stomach in and lifted her chin as they were shown into what looked like an elegant living room...it was that kind of place. A woman in a gold lamé sheath served them glasses of champagne with a smile that focused on Jason.

Sara's heart sank. He didn't need her help choosing anything here.

"Jason, darling!"

Sara stared at the woman who glided into the room and kissed Jason on the cheek. Her black gown, elbow-length gloves, and diamond earrings, made Sara wonder if the ties were going to be brought out on twenty-four karat gold trays. "How are you, *mon ami?* It has been so long."

"I'm fine, Gina. I've brought someone very special to meet you. My fiancée, Sara Adams. Sara, this is Gina Le Diamante, manager of Rudolfo's."

The woman turned and held both hands out to Sara. "What a pleasure, *mademoiselle*. Jason, she's a beauty, just as you said. My God, what bone structure. And those eyes ..."

Sara resisted the impulse to look over her shoulder. Who were they talking about?

"So, when can I come back?"

"About four?"

True, she was tired because she'd stayed up most of the night worrying about Jason and Kelsey, and even Dee-dee, but Sara knew she wasn't that fuzzy that she had missed something important. Jason intended leaving her with this woman. And she didn't know why.

A feeling of desperation shot up her spine and flooded her brain.

Slipping a hand through his arm and avoiding looking at him, Sara said, "Would you excuse us for a few moments, *madame?* I have something I must say to *darling* Jason before he leaves."

His body stiffened at the artificial emphasis on the endearment.

"Why of course, *mademoiselle.*" Gina Le Diamante's dark amused gaze slipped from Sara's face to Jason's. "You are young. You are in love. You must have privacy for your leave-taking. I will be back in a few minutes."

"What is going on here?" Sara snapped, as soon as the woman had glided out of the room.

"Gina is going to help you fix your hair and select a few things."

"Did it occur to you that I might like to be asked first, that I might not be able to pay for the things Gina selects? I'm not sure even the air in here doesn't have a price tag attached to it."

Jason actually looked taken aback. "I thought you'd like the surprise. Di—I mean, most women love shopping and being fussed over."

"I'm not most women," Sara said briskly. "I'm sorry if I've embarrassed you, but apologize to your friend for me, will you? I'll wait outside."

"Sara, wait!" He caught her by the arm, and she turned to face him. "I want you to get yourself some nice things. I'm going to pay for them. Dee-dee is very observant and you can't wear the same things day in and day out when she's here."

Sara's face flamed. Of course Jason didn't want Dee-dee to guess that she was just a poor employee. How could she have been so dense? Back to square one. It was all part of her job, as Jason had told her before.

"Well, maybe I'll get a couple of things," Sara said stiffly. Once Jason was gone, she would just ask Gina to show her the least expensive things in the store.

"That's my girl," Jason said, leaning down to brush her lips with his. "Gina's watching," he whispered close to her mouth.

The quick caress, the warm tickle of his words across her mouth, had Sara's heart beating so fast she barely heard Gina say, "Ah! Young love! It is so wonderful. But come, *mademoiselle,* we have much to accomplish."

Sara wet her lips. "I only want a couple of dresses," she said as she trailed beside Gina down a corridor that looked as if it belonged in a palace.

The Frenchwoman stopped short and looked at her. "Surely you joke, *mademoiselle.* Jason, he paid for a day of beauty for you here at Rudolfo's and I am to help you choose a complete wardrobe."

"A day of beauty?"

Gina nodded enthusiastically. "The—how you say in America?—the complete make-over. Facial, body massage, hairstyle, manicure, pedicure."

Did it come with a guarantee that Jason's money would be refunded when they realized that nothing could change this ugly duckling into a swan?

"Relax, *mademoiselle.* You will enjoy yourself. Your fiancé...he is so thoughtful. My husband should take lessons from him. Now come, change into this silk wrapper and then I will introduce you to Geronimo. He is a genius with hair."

Sara wondered if there was a patron saint of plain Janes she could appeal to before it was too late.

Four hours later, her skin tingling from all the attention it had received, Sara was led into a dressing room, the size of Uncle Samuel's living room.

Gina talked to her as models drifted in and out showing clothes Gina had selected for her. Sara picked out two pairs of silk pants and four tops as casual wear, and allowed Gina to convince her she needed two evening dresses right away. Nothing more.

"But Jason won't be happy," Gina argued.

"*Madame*, I am your customer," Sara said firmly. "Concentrate on making me happy. I'd also like to see some ties for men before I leave."

Gina nodded, and Sara felt a small thrill of victory. Had they scrubbed off that top layer of shyness that had always prevented her from saying what was on her mind?

An assistant brought in one of the gowns Sara had chosen. It was slipped over her head and then Gina turned her toward an ornate gilt mirror that took up most of one wall.

"Look, *mademoiselle*."

Sara stared. That wasn't her in the mirror.

The woman who stared back at her was someone exotic, someone as far removed from plain Sara Adams of Rainbow Valley as earth from sky. The lines of the classic off-the-shoulder, red floor-length dress made her look taller. The hairdresser had cut a wispy fringe that drew attention to her eyes. Skillful makeup and what she wore made her look quite different.

"You could be a model if you wished to, *mademoiselle*," the assistant who had helped slip the froth of red silk over her head said. "You are gorgeous."

"Please call me Sara." She had to hold on to the old, the ordinary, before her head floated away into the clouds.

Ties were brought in for her selection and Sara picked out three. As the assistant left to pack them, the room was filled with people carrying lamps and a man whose hair was half pink and half gone. A earring dangled from one ear, a cigarette from his mouth.

"Sara, this is Ramon. He is a very, very gifted photographer. I will be back when he's done." Gina took a look at Sara's face and said, "Your fiancé wants pictures of you."

Ramon and his helpers left half an hour later, telling her she was exquisite. Hoping that was the end of her day here, Sara turned back to the mirror for one last look.

They'd actually managed to cover up all her freckles. Would Jason think all the money he'd spent on her had been worth it? It would serve him right if he went into cardiac arrest when he saw the bill. They would probably take his house and his car and his company when they found out he couldn't pay.

At exactly five minutes to four, Jason returned to Rudolfo's. Had Sara enjoyed her day here? For a minute this morning he had thought Sara was going to walk out on him.

He'd made the remark about Dee-dee this morning out of sheer desperation. He was beginning to recognize the stubborn glow that came into Sara's eyes, the same way he recognized Kelsey's habit of sticking out her bottom lip.

"This way, *m'sieu.*" The woman held a velvet curtain aside, and Jason walked into the room.

His gaze went to the woman in front of the mirror. She had a beautiful back, emphasized by the way the red silk of her gown was draped low across it. He lifted his gaze to the face reflected in the mirror and his heartbeat quickened.

"Sara?"

She didn't say anything, simply stared at him through the mirror, and he went nearer. Never in his wildest dreams could he have imagined her looking like this. Her hair had been swept up in a new style, her eyes looked enormous, her red mouth an invitation he couldn't resist.

"You look beautiful." Putting a hand on her shoulder, he bent and touched his mouth to the bare skin of her shoulder as if to reassure himself this really was Sara. She jumped, but didn't move away.

"You like it?" The voice was the same.

Uncertain, timid, seeking.

"I love it." He lifted his other hand and touched the tip of one long dangling earring. Sara had an incredibly beautiful neck and he wanted to take her somewhere quiet and private to nibble on it. His gaze swept the way the silk clung to her breasts, defined her tiny waist and then flowed to the floor.

"This isn't really me."

His grasp on her shoulder tightened. "This isn't a part of you that you're used to, but this was always a part of you, waiting to be discovered. You can't hide from it any longer. This is the part I wanted you to see, Sara. Now do you believe what I said that day at Burnham Beeches? You've got eyes a man can both lose and find himself in."

He'd known she was beautiful, but her cool elegance surprised him.

Tension throbbed between them as they looked at each other in the mirror. Jason made no effort to hide the longing in his eyes.

I want you Sara. You're beautiful.

She seemed to sense his need because she turned to him, searching his face. Jason couldn't help himself. Cupping her face with both hands, he took her mouth. He kissed her leisurely, as he'd always wanted to, coaxing her lips apart, teasing her tongue till it reached out to explore his own mouth.

"A mouth made for kissing," he said huskily as he lifted his head.

"Ahem!" The sound at the door had them both turning to it. Jason looked at the young man who came in.

"Jason, this is Geronimo," he heard Sara say. "He did my hair."

"It was a pleasure to work with someone so beautiful, *mademoiselle*. Here are the packets that will help keep your hair as soft as silk."

"Thank you, Geronimo." There was a special softness about Sara's smile as she looked at the young man, and a curl of anger flared in Jason.

"Thank *you*, *mademoiselle*." Lifting one of Sara's hands, the young man pressed his mouth against it and then looked into her eyes as if he were a sick puppy. "If you need anything... anything at all, you only have to call me. My work and home phone number are on that card, and I will be happy to do anything for you."

Jason's fists clenched as the man left the room.

"Ah, there you are, *mon ami!*" Gina slid into the room and smiled at Jason. "Are you pleased?"

"Very." Jason tried to fight the feeling that maybe this had all been a mistake. He didn't want other men staring at Sara as if they wanted to take her home with them.

"The photographer said the pictures will be delivered to the flat in a day. He says if *mademoiselle* is interested in a modeling job, he can recommend an agency."

"She is not."

Gina looked amused. "I told him so already," she said smoothly. "A few of Sara's things have been put in your car. The rest will be sent to your home."

"Thank you, Gina."

Sara told herself she should have known that at Rudolfo's important customers weren't presented with anything as common as a bill before they left. It was probably slipped into a gold foil envelope and delivered by a winged messenger to their home addresses.

Jason turned to her again and said, "You look great. Wait till Dee-dee sees you. Plain and ordinary, ha!"

Her balloon of happiness burst so quickly, Sara wasn't sure she'd ever had one. Of course, this was all to impress Dee-dee and to convince her that Sara was genuine fiancée material. All part of her job, nothing more.

Cupping Sara's elbow, Jason steered her out of the salon. "Where are we going?" she asked Jason as a uniformed driver held open the rear door of a shiny black limo waiting at the curb. As she seated herself on the plush leather, she couldn't help but wonder what had happened to his car? Maybe this was part of the crash course in Personal Enhancement 101 she had to have before Dee-dee arrived.

"You'll see."

Jason cursed himself. Sara had changed the minute he'd mentioned Dee-dee. He had opened his mouth so wide that he'd stuffed both his size eleven feet into it. Settling in beside her, he watched Sara's profile as she stared out the window.

"Tired?"

"A little."

"I have something for you."

Sara stared at the box he handed her. "Open it."

Another ring? Or maybe this time it was a tiara. That might just about impress Dee-dee. Close to tears, and not sure why, Sara lifted the lid of the eight-by-four box.

She picked up the envelope inside and stared at the tickets. "Tickets to Swan Lake? For tonight? Oh, Jason!"

His heart lifted. It was the first real note of happiness he had heard in her voice all day. "Oh, Sara!"

The teasing note in his voice made her blush. "You shouldn't spend all this money on me."

"I got the tickets cheap. Would you like to go?"

She nodded, but a frown pleated her brow a second later. "What's wrong?"

"I've hardly seen Kelsey all day," she said. "Do you think we could stop by the apartment for a few minutes?"

Jason shot her a surprised glance. He should know by now that Kelsey always came first with Sara. "Kelsey's fine. Mrs. Binty thought you might be worrying about her and she sent a message."

"What is it?"

"She said you're to enjoy the evening and not fash yourself with worry, whatever 'fash yourself' means."

Jason took her to a small French bistro for dinner before the ballet. Excusing himself after they were seated, he picked up the suit bag he'd carried into the restaurant from the limo and said, "Be back in a minute."

The sight of him in a tux, a silky red bow tie that matched her dress exactly at his neck, made Sara stare. She'd never seen Jason look more handsome.

"I had to keep up with you," he said lightly in answer to the question in her eyes.

Confusion jumped in to share the space with a strange new excitement in Sara's mind. It was getting harder and harder to remember that she and Jason were just practicing their roles.

He persuaded her to try the quail in pastry with port sauce, and he had the lamb cutlets with crème of sweet pepper. Sara stopped objecting to anything; in fact she stopped looking at the prices on the menu . . . if this was all part of her education there was nothing she could do.

She noticed that Jason became increasingly quiet as they ate. Maybe her freckles were showing and he was regretting the huge amount of money he'd been forced to spend on her?

He looked up and their gazes tangled. "I called Dee-dee and invited her to stay with us."

Sara's fork slipped from her hand, landing with a little clatter on her plate. "You did what?"

"I followed your advice, but if she sets one foot wrong she's going to be out of that apartment before you can say grandmother."

Sara stared at him. "What made you do that?"

"I thought about what you said. Maybe if she does see Kelsey and me together, it will change her mind. I've tried everything else, I might as well give your way a shot."

It would be her fault if it didn't work out.

Sara picked up her fork, hoping that she hadn't been wrong about the look of love she'd seen in Dee-dee's eyes when she'd looked at Kelsey.

She knew how much it must have taken for Jason to make the offer. Having Dee-dee stay at the apartment would be like opening up a vein. The constant reminders of his wife would be hard on him. It only proved that Jason would go to any lengths for Kelsey.

Sara picked up a glass of water and tried to swallow the lump in her throat. She had to play her part right.

At the ballet, Jason watched Sara more than he watched the stage. The famous dancers were impressive, but he would have given anything to be able to capture the expressions on Sara's face as she watched them.

Engrossed in the story, she was oblivious of him. The tears on her cheeks as the story unfolded created a strange ache in his chest. He wanted to put his arms around Sara, tell her that it was only make-believe, that real life was happier. The need shook Jason with its intensity. He had never felt this way about Diana.

Sara didn't want to talk on the way home and Jason was content with the way she sat close to him. "That was beautiful, Jason. Thank you."

He put an arm around her shoulders and tucked her into his side. "Would you like a liqueur?"

"No, thank you."

He poured himself a crème de menthe from the bar in the limo, and sipped it. "Try it," he said, holding the crystal liqueur glass up.

Sara sipped it, her gaze tangling with his. Jason set the glass down and reached for her. Her mouth met his with an urgency that surprised him. She raised her hands and placed them on his shoulders, urging him closer. Jason's mouth left hers long enough to trail down the side of her neck and then return to her soft lips again.

His hands caressed her slim shoulders and then his thumbs traced the neckline of her dress just where the gentle swell of her breasts began.

"Sara," he murmured against her lips.

The sound of his voice reminded her that they were in a limo, that any minute now it was going to pull up at The Towers.

Sara pulled away from Jason as he reached for her again. This was madness. She couldn't give in to it.

"Sara, it's all right."

"No, Jason."

She knew what he meant. They could turn the fake engagement into a reality, get married. Only it would never be all right because accepting a business marriage would mean surrendering her dreams. Passion couldn't take the place of love. "I still want my freedom."

He drew away from her as if she had slapped him. Sitting back in his corner, he ran a hand through his hair and looked out the window on his side.

A thousand explanations tumbled around in Sara's head, but she couldn't voice any. Her heart beat too fast and she was desperately afraid that she couldn't control what she felt for Jason Graham.

Chapter Eight

He didn't see her in the morning before he left for work. Was Sara sleeping in, or avoiding him?

"Miss Sara offered to go to the market for me this morning," Mrs. Binty told him as she made his breakfast. "Don't know why, because she can't tell the difference between monkfish and plaice."

She was avoiding him. Jason's heart sank. Forcing Sara to take this job, by threatening to complain about her friend, had been bad enough. Did she feel that he was threatening her in a more personal way now?

He had to find a way to let Sara know that she had a right to try her new wings.

Dee-dee arrived Wednesday night, a few minutes after Jason got home from a four-hour meeting. She hugged Kelsey, cast Sara a quick look, and said, "You look different."

Sara resisted the impulse to tug at the neckline of the peacock blue silk blouse she wore. It was one of the new ones, lower in front than she was used to.

"Did you have a good journey? Kelsey's been waiting for her grandma." She picked up Dee-dee's hand luggage and smiled at her. "You must be tired. Let me show you to your room."

Dee-dee looked startled by the warmth of Sara's welcome. "Well... I am a bit tired."

Sara stole a quick look at Jason. His expression told her nothing. "Mrs. Binty's got a nice dinner waiting. Would you like a tray in your room? Kelsey and I were worn out after our trip here. Jason, honey, I'll be right back."

Jason *honey's* eyes narrowed dangerously before he said, "Right."

The sight of Sara with her hair loose about her shoulders, smiling at him as if she loved him, disturbed him. The blue jeans hugged the curves of her bottom, and the neck of the blouse gave him a glimpse of the figure usually hidden under skirts and long sweaters.

The words "Jason, honey" had been a surprise. They'd also been a reminder of how easily women could change. Diana had. And Sara had proven that she could play a number of roles well. Was her other role—that of a shy, self-effacing woman—an act, too?

The sight of Dee-dee had upset him. Jason's temper rose as the cabdriver brought in all her luggage. Two designer shopping bags were filled with toys that Kelsey didn't need.

Sara had whisked Dee-dee away quickly, which was a good thing, because if she said or did one thing to upset anyone, she was leaving, and he didn't want to throw her out tonight.

Jason picked up his briefcase and headed for his room. Kelsey had left the room with Sara and Dee-dee and he could hear the murmur of voices from the guest room. He caught a glimpse of a vase of flowers on Dee-dee's dresser as he passed the open door and knew Sara had put it there. He only hoped she would be strong enough to cope with Dee-dee in the days to come.

Forty-eight hours later Jason was hoping *he* would be strong enough to cope. Not with Dee-dee, who was strangely quiet around him, but with Sara, who'd thrown herself wholeheartedly into the role of fiancée.

It had been a month since he'd met Sara. A month in which he'd steadily lost all control of the situation. Her hello and goodbye kisses heated his blood and confused his thinking. Tonight she'd gotten up from the dinner table to get a special hot sauce for Dee-dee, and her hand had rested on his shoulder. The smile she'd given him had been warm, only her eyes had been expressionless as she'd looked into his.

Jason didn't know how to handle the way he felt about her. He'd ruthlessly subdued his first impulse to take her somewhere quiet where he could kiss her as he wanted to and tell her that she'd touched a part of him no one ever had.

Telling her would not be wise, though. There was no way he was going to let history repeat itself. Sara must never feel, like Di had, that he'd coerced her into anything. If freedom was what she wanted, freedom was what she had to have.

His first plan that he would give her six months of living on her own before he proposed didn't seem like such a sound one now. Sara seemed to have changed so much in the time he'd known her. Her new clothes, her hair, even the light makeup she used, drew many admiring glances when they were out in public. Jason had to deal with a new fear: what if Sara fell in love with someone else while he waited in the wings?

Worry drove Jason to stay late at the office over the next few days, working harder than he ever had before to tie up all the legal aspects of the new deals he was making.

Sara couldn't understand the restlessness that snowballed inside her in the course of Dee-dee's visit. Having Dee-dee around gave her the excuse she needed to kiss Jason. She enjoyed the feel of his mouth against hers. Hot, sweet, *demanding*. This morning he had pulled her against him and claimed her mouth as if he would never let her go. The look of desire in Jason's eyes unnerved her. She was playing with fire, and if she wasn't careful, it would burn her.

"Are you sure you'll be all right with Dee-dee?" Jason asked Sara. He'd stayed at the apartment, hoping to find a way of talking to Sara alone. Instead he'd received a phone call midmorning that made it necessary to go to a meeting in Paris. Twin prongs of indecision and worry had gripped him. "This trip's come up so suddenly there's nothing I can do about it. I'll be back tomorrow night."

There was no way to postpone the trip without risking losing a big new deal, but leaving Sara with Dee-dee made him feel he was abandoning the little brown owl to an eagle. Jason recognized the signs in his household. Even-tempered Mrs. Binty had looked upset the last day or two, and Mr. Binty had asked him privately how long Dee-dee would be staying. Dee-dee was doing what she always did best—rubbing everyone the wrong way.

"I'll be fine," Sara said.

"How are you and Dee-dee getting along?"

"We're doing fine."

The answer came a little too quick. Jason reached out and took Sara's chin in his hand. "Sara, look at me. I don't want you to have to put up with any nonsense. Remember the terms of our contract? I don't want you hiding anything from me."

She wrenched out of his grasp. "Don't worry about it, Jason. I told you, everything's fine."

Sara fought the strangest feeling of desolation welling inside as she watched Jason leave. Without an audience there had been no need for them to kiss goodbye.

The next day dragged. She encouraged Dee-dee to accompany Kelsey and Mrs. Binty to the park, and she tried to concentrate on her writing. Half an hour of staring at a blank page of paper and she gave up.

Jason had taken over her mind and her heart. Longing flooded her to feel his arms around her again, to be kissed, to watch that incredible molten heat in Jason's eyes.

Sara got to her feet, knocking her notebook to the floor in her hurry. *Stop making a total idiot of yourself.* Picking the book up, she decided to go and check on the soup Mrs. Binty had left simmering on the stove.

She hadn't expected to miss Jason so much. Neither had she expected to wake up today with this feeling of excitement inside, telling her she was glad about his return. For his sake and Kelsey's, she'd hoped having Dee-dee here would mend some fences.

It wasn't easy. Dee-dee had a knack for upsetting people without even trying. Her insistent questions about Kelsey's routine had upset Mrs. Binty and she persisted in telling Sara how happy Jason and her Diana had been, how it was impossible for Jason to ever love like that again.

Was that why Jason had wanted to marry her? Because Sara Adams would be undemanding and fill the slot of wife and mother without expecting too much of him?

A tiny spark of rebellion flared in Sara's breast. She was done with being a doormat—of any kind. Maybe it was insane to want to be loved just for herself, but it was one area where she wasn't accepting any half measures. If she couldn't have it all, she would opt for nothing, however hard that was.

She was in the living room with Kelsey that night, reading a story about a family. When she came to the end of it, Sara said, "Kelsey's got so many people in her family. Daddy and Sara and Grandma. Mr. and Mrs. Binty. Let's see how many people those are. One, two, three, four, five."

She looked up at a sound near the doorway. Dee-dee stood there looking as if she'd seen a ghost. Without a word, she turned away, and Sara sighed. Maybe the picture she'd drawn had hurt Dee-dee by reminding her that Sara was usurping her daughter's rightful place.

When she went to bed at eleven, Jason still hadn't come in.

The next morning, when Sara came out to have breakfast, carrying Kelsey, she thought he had left for work, but he was at the breakfast table.

"Hello, Sara!" Getting up, he hugged and kissed Kelsey. Sara was so glad to see him that she just stared at him, taking in everything about his appearance. She'd missed him so much.

"Jason, I didn't hear you come in last night," Dee-dee said as she bustled into the room and poured herself a cup of coffee. The inquisitive way she turned and looked at her reminded Sara that she hadn't said anything.

"Jason!" Sara put Kelsey down and launched herself at him, placing her arms around him and burying her face in his chest. "It's so good to have you back."

She lifted her face, surprised when Jason bent and kissed her taking his time about it. Warmth enveloped her inside out and she wanted to melt.

It's all part of the job, Sara told herself as her mouth opened under the pressure of Jason's lips. *It's all part of the job.*

"I missed you."

She stared at him in wonder as he released her gently and sat back down, lifting Kelsey onto his lap. There had been nothing in his eyes to show the words were part of their act.

"I missed you, too. Why didn't you wake me up when you got in?"

"There was no point in it. It was 3:00 a.m. and you looked exhausted."

He had looked in on her? Sara felt the color in her face deepen. Hopefully her freckles weren't the glow-in-the dark kind, and she hadn't been snoring.

Sara turned to Dee-dee, taken aback by the way Kelsey's grandmother was studying her. "Well, Mrs. Binty's at the market, Mr. Binty's picking up Jason's clothes from the cleaners. And Kelsey and I are going to the park."

At the word "park," Kelsey scrambled off Jason's lap and hurried to her room to get the light cotton jacket Mrs. Binty always put on her. Returning, she held it out to Sara, who helped her slip it on and watched her button it. "You're a good girl for Grandma, okay, sweetheart?"

Kelsey nodded and gave Sara a kiss on the mouth before turning to do the same for her father.

"We'll be back at eleven," Dee-dee said as they walked out the door.

"Was she trying to tell us something?" Jason asked.

"I think she was just trying to give us some time together."

Jason frowned. And he was born yesterday.

"Sit down and eat."

Sara sat and helped herself to some oatmeal from the dish Mrs. Binty had left on the table.

"So, how have things been here?"

"We've been fine. How was your trip?"

Jason was not to be sidetracked. "Has Dee-dee been making a nuisance of herself?"

"No. We've been getting along fine—"

"I forgot to get some tissues." Dee-dee walked over to the counter, pulled five out of the box and stuck them into the pocket of her jacket. "There, we're all set now."

Still holding Kelsey's hand, she walked out as Kelsey waved to them.

Sara bit her lip. Had Dee-dee heard them discussing her?

As the front door closed, Sara looked at Jason. "Deep down she's very lonely, Jason. Give her a chance."

He looked as if a bolt of lightning had struck him. "Me? She's the one who's taking me to court. She's the one who wants to take Kelsey away from me."

"She lost a daughter...her only child. Kelsey's all she has left of Diana." There, she'd actually said the woman's name out loud to Jason. "She's afraid."

"Sara..."

"Let me finish, please." She couldn't get her courage up like this till next year. "Jason, Dee-dee hasn't mentioned the case once since she got here. Can't you forget the case, forget everything, and just treat Dee-dee as if she's Kelsey's grandmother here for a visit?"

He pushed his chair away from the table, but didn't get up. "You're asking a lot, Sara. Dee-dee isn't about to change, no matter what I do."

Sara didn't believe that. "Kelsey's going to be the real loser in this battle. Have you thought that she might like to have a grandmother around as she's growing up? There'll come a time when she'll want to know about Diana, and who better to tell her than Dee-dee? You don't like talking about her, and Kelsey's entitled to know about her mother."

The look in Jason's eyes made Sara say quickly, "I understand perfectly why it's so hard for you. I mean, you loved Diana and..." Her voice trailed away when she saw the way Jason's face darkened.

"I loved Diana when I married her. I stopped loving her when I realized Diana had never loved me, just the man she'd thought she could turn me into."

Sara swallowed. The tightness around Jason's mouth told her how hard it was for him to discuss his wife.

"I'm sorry. It's none of my business, really, but family's important."

Family's important.

The words tore at Jason. He had no right to deny his daughter's ties with her mother's family.

The worried look in Sara's eyes made him touch her on the shoulder. "Maybe you're right. Maybe I have been looking at this from the wrong angle. I'm willing to give your way a try and be nicer to Dee-dee."

"You are?" Sara asked, dazed.

"Sara, I'm not the mean monster you think I am. What you said makes perfect sense. Why should Kelsey lose both her mother and her grandmother? I never knew my grandparents and I always used to watch the other kids in boarding school when theirs came to visit."

"You were in boarding school?"

"My dad was in the army and when my mother died and he remarried, my stepmother thought it was the best place for me."

Sara picked up the change in Jason's voice. Did he feel he'd been sent away? "Your stepmother and your father probably didn't want your education to be interrupted."

"They didn't want me around," Jason said harshly.

Was that another reason he had proposed to her? Meek and mild Sara Adams would never have the kind of influence over him that he thought his stepmother had had over his father.

"Were you very close to your father before he remarried?"

"Very."

Sara bit her lip. She was so far in, she might as well go all the way. "One of the girls I was at high school with lost three years of schooling because her parents were in the military. She said she couldn't adjust to changing school all the time and after a while she gave up trying to keep up with her schoolwork. She dropped out in her junior year of high school."

"What are you trying to say, Sara?"

"I think your stepmother didn't send you away, Jason. She really wanted what was best for you."

Jason frowned. Was what Sara said true?

"How old were you when your mother died, Jason?"

"Nine."

"Didn't she ever mention boarding school to you?"

The memory returned in a flash. His mother lighting the candles on his birthday cake. She'd bent and kissed his cheek after he'd cut it, and said, "I'll miss this when we go away to Germany and you're at school."

Fragments of memory came back. Yes, Mom had mentioned boarding school from time to time. It hadn't been only Margaret's idea. How could he have forgotten?

"They were going to Germany and I was going to boarding school," Jason said slowly. "I remember Mom mentioning it now."

Sara got to her feet and started clearing the table. "They didn't send you away on purpose."

After his mother had died, he'd hurt so badly. It had hurt even worse to know that Dad had wanted to marry someone else. He'd been too angry to listen to explanations, to believe what his father had said about loving him just as much as always. During vacations he had rejected Margaret's offers of friendship, grown up quiet and reserved. They had died in a car accident while he'd been away in college.

Jason stared at the kitchen wallpaper. If only he'd been a little more patient with his father. His mouth tightened. He couldn't rewrite the past, but he would give Dee-dee another chance.

"I want to do what's best for Kelsey."

He must have said it aloud, because Sara came and stood by him. Placing a hand on his shoulder, she said, "You always will, Jason. Every parent who loves his child does their best."

Jason put a hand up and held Sara's. He needed the comfort of her touch. "My dad did his best for me, only I didn't see it that way. He wrote to me after I went away to boarding school, telling me that I had a special place in his life that no one else could ever fill."

"Just like Kelsey has in your heart."

"If I lose Kelsey to Dee-dee, she might grow up to think that I didn't care enough to keep her with me. The only reason I've been taking her with me on these trips is because I never want her to feel abandoned the way I did as a child. I didn't know moving her around might affect her development."

It was the basis of Dee-dee's case, and because Kelsey hadn't started talking, Sara knew Jason must worry if it was true. Being a parent was never easy, especially when one had to make decisions like the kind Jason was faced with. The pain in his voice made Sara wrap both arms around him and hold his head to her chest the way she did with Kelsey.

"You're doing your best, Jason," she said fiercely, blinking to stop the tears falling. "No one can do more than that."

Sara went out for a long walk in the park that afternoon to think about what Jason had told her. The park was crowded because it was Sunday, but Sara hardly noticed the people.

Why did some people's lives hold so many jagged pieces that kept hurting them? Jason had wanted to do his best by his father. Was there a patron saint of single parents? Couldn't he, or she, see that Jason was doing more than his best, that all the man wanted was to be allowed to take care of his daughter?

Tears filled Sara's eyes, but she brushed them away. Her third challenge was to put her own feelings aside and concentrate on helping Jason as much as she could.

"Why do you and Jason have separate bedrooms?"

Jason paused on the balcony, his heart beginning to thud. Dee-dee's question was loaded with innuendo. Kelsey had gone to bed, and Jason had retired to his room on the pretext of work. Why had Sara gone to Dee-dee's room? It would have been simpler just to put her head into a crocodile's mouth.

"We have separate bedrooms because we've decided to wait until we're married to sleep together."

Sara must have rehearsed that answer in her mind for it to come out so pat.

"Hah! It's the first time Jason Graham's waited for anything."

Jason's mouth tightened as he waited for the volley of spite that would follow. The promise he'd given Sara wasn't going to be easy to keep.

Sara cleared her throat before she said, "Jason's past is his business."

"Not if it influences my granddaughter's upbringing." The vinegar Dee-dee had put on her salad was showing in her voice.

"As far as I know, a saint couldn't raise a child better than Jason is doing. Why do you keep treating him like some kind of criminal? Because your daughter died and Jason lived?"

"She would never have rushed out of the house that night on her own. He won't admit it, but they must have had a fight."

"You told Mrs. Binty that Jason was in England the night Diana died," Sara said calmly. "You also said that the autopsy showed that her blood alcohol level was very high that night."

"He drove her to drink."

"She started drinking after she married Jason?"

"No."

"When did she start?"

"In her teens."

"The truth is, you couldn't control Diana even then, could you, Dee-dee? No one could."

In the silence that followed, Jason realized that Sara would have made a great lawyer.

"It wasn't my fault that Diana was so wild."

"No one's blaming you, Dee-dee, but you've got to stop acting as if Jason's the one to blame. Diana was responsible for what happened to her. You knew your own daughter, and you know Jason. At least to yourself, can't you admit who was really at fault?"

Another silence, and then Sara said, "Don't let Kelsey suffer because you want to pin responsibility for your daughter's death on Jason."

"Diana didn't want to have Kelsey."

"But she did, and nothing can change that."

"Jason refused to let her have an abortion."

"In this day and age Diana could have gotten one if she'd really wanted to. The fact she didn't proves that deep down she, too, hoped the baby would change things.

"You need Kelsey as much as she needs you. If Jason wins the case—and he will—that's going to leave you out in the cold. You've lost your daughter, there's no need to lose your granddaughter, as well. Don't do what my uncle did. He shut love out of his life and made being unhappy a habit."

It was the first time Sara had volunteered information about Samuel Bly.

"Di was so wild...she would never listen to me. We spoiled her. I don't want Kelsey to turn out like that."

Jason wondered if Sara knew Dee-dee had never discussed her daughter like this with anyone.

"She won't. You don't see Jason spoiling her, do you? And you'll be on hand to make sure the mistakes that were made with Diana aren't repeated."

"Jason doesn't want me around."

"The fact he's invited you to stay here proves he's trying his best to accept that you're an important part of Kelsey's life. You'll always be her grandmother."

"Do you mean that? You won't shut me out once you're married?"

Through the gap in the billowing curtains, Jason saw Sara kneel in front of Dee-dee's armchair and take both her hands. "I didn't have a grandparent around when I grew up and I envied the kids who did. My best friend, Claire, could always talk to her grandmother about anything...she was one of her best friends. I want Kelsey to have the wealth of family."

A wealth she'd never had herself. Dee-dee said nothing and Sara got to her feet. "I'd better go finish putting the laundry away."

Jason couldn't understand the heaviness that banded his chest. Sara had pleaded his cause as if it were her own. Kelsey's future was very important to her.

"Himself wants to see you in his room, miss, when you have a moment free," Mr. Binty told Sara at ten Monday morning.

Sara smiled at Mr. Binty. She'd gotten used to the way both the Bintys addressed Jason as Himself. So far she hadn't been able to persuade them to drop the "miss" where she was concerned and call her Sara. It was just not their way.

Going to Jason's bedroom, Sara knocked on the open door.

"Sara, come in. I have to apologize. I opened one of your letters by mistake."

Sara glanced at the envelope in Jason's hand. Claire was the only person who bothered to write to her and Sara hoped Claire hadn't made any too euphoric references to Jason. "That's okay."

"This envelope was lying facedown. I was halfway through the letter when I realized it was for you."

Her eyes widened as she saw the return address printed on top of the page. It was from a nationally known writing magazine that sponsored an annual writing contest. She'd given Claire's address when she'd entered the contest and her friend had forwarded it. Sara's hands shook as she extracted the single sheet of paper. As she read the words on the page, her heart seemed to stop for a single second and then break into a gallop.

She'd won first place in the essay competition. There had been one hundred entrants in the category she'd entered. One of the judges was the editor of a national magazine and he wanted to publish her essay.

Sara raised her gaze to Jason's, still unable to take it all in. Why on earth was he looking at her so strangely?

"Congratulations."

"I e-entered this competition some time back. I n-never expected to win."

"You're a good writer, Sara, and this is proof. You could call the editor who wants to publish you from here if you'd like to."

The idea seemed to petrify her. "C-call the editor?" she said in a tone that implied he'd suggested calling St. Peter in heaven. "I'll think about it, thank you."

She turned and left the room.

He'd wanted her to experience freedom the way he imagined it to be, to gain confidence in herself. He'd done everything to give it to her, but that wasn't the best way. This was the best way... gaining it through her own accomplishments. Winning the competition opened up a whole new world for Sara.

Getting to his feet, Jason reached for the phone on his desk. He had to stop being selfish about letting Sara go.

"You actually won a competition?" he heard Mr. Binty say as he entered the kitchen ten minutes later. "How clever of you, miss!"

Mrs. Binty beamed proudly at Sara. "So it's a writer you are, are ye? I thought to myself when I saw those papers all over that you were working very hard at something."

Sara smiled. The idea was taking some getting used to. She'd shared her news with the Bintys and Dee-dee, because saying it out loud helped her believe in it herself.

"What does Jason have to say about all this?" Dee-dee asked. "He never mentioned that you write."

Before Sara could answer Jason walked up to her and slipped an arm around her waist. "Jason thinks it's wonderful. Sara didn't want to discuss her writing with anyone because it was a dream too close to her heart to share. Exposure has a way of destroying budding hopes."

Sara felt herself stiffen with surprise. Jason had said that as if he were looking through a keyhole right into her mind.

The doorbell rang, and Kelsey and Mr. Binty went to answer it. When they returned, Mr. Binty held two dozen roses in his hand. Kelsey handed her a card.

"For me?" Sara opened it.

> Congratulations, Sara.
> Success belongs to people like you who dare to dream and then work toward putting foundations under their dreams.

It was signed "Jason and Kelsey." He must have ordered them from the florist downstairs.

Sara looked at him as he took the flowers from Mr. Binty and put them into her hands. "We're so proud of you, Sara."

She buried her face in the roses, and then held the roses for Kelsey to sniff. "They're wonderful. Th-thank you, Jason."

Sara wasn't aware she sounded lukewarm till she glanced at Mrs. Binty and Dee-dee. They were both looking at her strangely. Instinct told her she wasn't reacting the way she ought to.

She'd just received amazing news. Her fiancé had done something romantic and generous. She'd thanked him as if they were strangers. It didn't add up right. Sara put the flowers on the table, and placed both hands on Jason's shoulders.

Jason didn't know if it was the pressure of Sara's fingers on his shoulders, urging him to bend down so she could brush her lips against his, or the shy look that only he could see that came into her eyes every time she kissed him, that heated his blood. Maybe it was the fact that soon she'd want to spread her wings and fly right out of his life.

He hauled her to his chest and crushed her mouth under his. His tongue plunged into the soft cavern of her moistness and when he lifted his head, they were both breathing hard and there was no sign of anyone else in the kitchen.

Sara stared up at Jason. Her heart felt as if it were going to burst and her legs shook so badly if she pulled away from him she thought she might fall.

That had been more than a play-acting kiss.

Jason reached up and brushed aside a strand of hair that had fallen across her lips. "Go and get dressed. We're going out to dinner to celebrate the fact you're a soon-to-be-published author. Shall we leave at seven?"

"There's no need to celebrate. I mean, it's not as if I'm published, or anything like that."

The finger on her lips stopped her. "Sara, the letter you just received is a milestone in your life as a writer. We have to make the day memorable."

The tears came so fast, she wasn't prepared for them. Suddenly they were wetting her cheeks, pouring out as if they would never stop.

"What's wrong?"

She couldn't say a word. Busy trying to stop them, she wiped them away, but fresh ones followed.

Jason reached for her and took her into his arms. Cradling her head, he pressed it to his chest and let his lips rest against her forehead. "Shh! It's all right. It's all right."

Her slender body shook with the force of her tears and it was a while before she got to the hiccuping stage.

"Want to sit down and let me get you a cup of tea?"

She shook her head, tightening her hold around his middle. Heat flowed through Jason.

"Was it something I said?"

Her head moved up and down against his wet shirtfront. Jason thought about it. All he'd done was get her a small bunch of flowers and congratulate her. His jaw clenched. Had anyone ever celebrated Sara's victories?

He didn't think so. Holding Sara's arms, he stepped away from her. The sight of her red eyes and nose made him want to kiss her again.

"We're going to paint London red tonight."

Sara sniffed. "We don't have to go out. I'll tell them I want to stay right here and celebrate."

"We'll do that tomorrow night," Jason said. "Tonight I want you to myself."

Sara stood in the middle of the kitchen after Jason left, wondering if there was anything wrong with her hearing.

Had Jason really said "I want you to myself"?

The memory of the kiss they'd exchanged earlier escalated the heat pooling in her stomach. Had he noticed the suspicious looks Dee-dee had been giving them recently? Was the kiss his way of emphasizing to Dee-dee that they were madly in love?

Sara looked at the clock. She'd better hurry. She wanted to reply to her letter before she went out, and she wasn't sure how long it was going to take to put her makeup on. A part of her wanted to see the same light in Jason's eyes that she had when he'd come to pick her up at Rudolfo's.

Chapter Nine

Jason was knotting his tie when he heard a knock on the door. "Come in," he threw over his shoulder.

It was Dee-dee. "I want to talk with you, if you have a minute?"

Surprise held Jason quiet for a few seconds. Dee-dee wanted to talk to him? She looked as if she'd been crying, and she was twisting her hands.

"Sure. Come on in and sit down."

She took the only armchair in the room and he wheeled the chair around from his computer desk and sat on it.

"I've decided to go home tomorrow and I wanted to thank you for letting me stay here this week." Dee-dee sounded as if she were about to cry again. "I just wanted to tell you that I'll be dropping the custody case."

Deep relief welled up in him. Sara had done this. "Thank you, Dee-dee."

"Sara said that you wouldn't mind me visiting Kelsey. I p-promise to call first."

"Of course not." Sara had taught him about being generous. "In fact, I might have to return to England in September. I'll just be here three days, so there's no point in having Kelsey make the trip. Maybe you'd like to have her come stay with you during that time, or you could stay at our place?"

Dee-dee's eyes looked as if they might pop right out of her head. "You mean that?"

"I do."

"Oh, Jason, I'm so sorry for all those things I said about you." Dee-dee buried her face in the tissue in her hands. Her sobs reverberated in the silent room. "I—I've made so many mistakes. I knew how selfish and spoiled Di was, and yet I blamed you for everything."

Jason patted her back awkwardly. "I made some mistakes, too. We can only do our best as human beings, Dee-dee. Don't worry about the past."

She reached up suddenly and kissed him. "You're a good man, Jason, and I'm glad you've found Sara. Sara will heal all the pain of the past. She made me see how important I am to Kelsey. I was so scared after Diana died and you began to travel. At the time I thought you were deliberately keeping Kelsey away from me."

He could afford being generous in victory. "I was wrong, too. I should have explained things to you, but I was hurting badly. I never wanted to keep Kelsey away from you. You're part of our family."

"Do you really mean that, Jason? Things won't change after you and Sara marry?"

"You know Sara. Do you think she'll change?"

Dee-dee's face lightened. "No, I don't think she will. Sara's a good person."

"I do want to make a few things very clear." He'd better speak his piece while Dee-dee was in a listening mode.

"I know the rules," Dee-dee said quickly. "I'm not buying Kelsey any new toys or clothes without checking with Sara first. No junk food and no candy when she's out with me. Anything else?"

"I can't think of anything," Jason said reluctantly. He'd be lucky if Dee-dee kept twenty-five percent of her promise.

"Thank you, Jason, for giving me another chance." Dee-dee stopped at the door and turned. "Mrs. Binty and I are taking Kelsey shopping tomorrow before I leave. The poor child needs a new jacket . . . hers has a stain on it."

Jason sighed. A month ago the same statement would have made him furious and resentful. He would have seen it as a criticism of his parental abilities, now he saw it as Dee-dee's way.

"Just don't make it mink," he called after her.

Jason turned his attention back to his tie. It was one of the new ties that had arrived with Sara's things from Rudolfo's. He liked the conservative gray and blue design on a black background. Sara, as usual, had known he wouldn't like anything too flashy.

Things had worked out better than he'd expected. He had gotten exactly what he wanted—unchallenged custody of his daughter—without having to go through an ugly court battle. He would be on top of the world—except for one thing. Jason adjusted the knot at his neck. He no longer had a reason to employ Sara. The thought filled him with emptiness.

Sara will heal all the pain of the past. Had Dee-dee seen how much he loved Sara; that the longing in his eyes was real? He'd have to be very careful that Sara didn't guess how he felt. She had a right to try her wings, experience the joy of flying.

The great hunger that was his love for Sara seemed to grow bigger every day. Now that there was no need for them to keep up this charade, he should set Sara free as soon as possible. Her new life was waiting for her and she had a right to know.

His mind balked at telling her right away. They still had two weeks left in England. What harm would it do to keep her with them that much longer?

To himself, Jason admitted he was going to listen to the small voice inside him that said maybe, just maybe, in the next few days Sara would decide to love him back.

The tiny sound woke Jason at about 2:00 a.m. Out of habit he was on his feet, pulling on a shirt as he went toward Kelsey's room. He saw Sara right away. She sat in the chair by the window, crooning one of her soft melodies.

She hadn't changed out of the blue dress she had worn that evening. Jason took a look at Kelsey's face. She was fast asleep.

"What's wrong?" he whispered, placing the back of his hand against his daughter's cheek. To his relief, her skin felt normal to his touch.

"She must have had a bad dream. I heard her whimpering and I came out to pick her up."

"You haven't been to bed?"

"I couldn't sleep."

She'd sat by her window, staring out at the shadow of the trees in the park, trying to analyze her feelings. The evening with Jason had been perfect. They'd seen a really funny play and then had dinner at the bistro that was becoming her favorite place to eat. Jason had ordered champagne and insisted she try some. He'd been charming and attentive, and Sara had been deeply disappointed that he hadn't made any move to kiss her good-night.

The evening had played on her tightly strung emotions. The new awareness that hung between them seemed more potent than ever. At times Sara had felt Jason wanted her to say something, only she didn't know what, or how to say it.

Sara had given in to the impulse to reach up and grab the white scarf that he'd worn with his dark jacket. Yanking his mouth lightly toward her, she murmured against his lips, "Dee-dee might be still up."

He'd taken over the kiss as he'd done earlier. Only this time when it was over, he'd left without a word. She hadn't gone to bed because she'd known she wouldn't be able to sleep. Jason's rejection of her had been unmistakable.

"Want me to take her?" Crouched beside the chair, his breath was a warm whisper against Sara's cheek.

"No, that's fine," Sara whispered back. "She's just settled down. I don't want her to wake up again."

Which made perfect sense. Jason took the window seat, and Sara protested, "You don't have to stay up. I'll put her down in ten minutes."

"I want to stay, Sara." The half-light in the room seemed to give him courage for some of the things he had to say.

All evening he had tried to show Sara how important she was to him, but only the fact that he couldn't deprive her of the freedom that beckoned held Jason back. He wasn't going to be the one who took that freedom away from her.

Sara's heart leapt as she recalled the first time they had stayed up together because Kelsey'd had a bad dream. They'd come a long way since then. Maybe Jason was going to discuss what was happening between them.

"I can never thank you enough for all the things you've done for Kelsey and me. I will always be in your debt. If there's anything I can do for you in return, don't hesitate to let me know."

The cold came up from her toes all the way to her heart. Tiredness swept over Sara. "Thank you, Jason."

He was already pointing out that this job was over. Standing up, Sara took one step toward the crib and stopped. Her right foot was completely numb.

"What is it?" Jason was beside her in a moment.

"Will you take her, please? My right foot's fallen asleep."

The back of his hand brushed against her breast as he took his daughter. Sara felt a tongue of responsive warmth dart through her cold body. Sitting back in the chair, she began to rub her foot.

"Let me do that." Jason knelt on the floor in front of her and took her foot in his hands. The feel of his thumbs against the sole of her foot made Sara feel she was melting inside.

Jason put a hand up and began to squeeze her calf. "Are you taking any vitamins, Sara?" he asked.

Vitamins? What on earth he was talking about? She was burning up with longing and all he could think of was vitamins.

"I'll get you some tomorrow. You're much too thin and you work too hard."

"I'll get them myself," Sara snapped.

She didn't want him getting her vitamins in gold or platinum foil capsules from Rudolfo's, if any such thing existed.

The feel of Sara's skin was driving him crazy. He'd barely been able to walk away when she'd kissed him. Now the feeling he'd reined in earlier had cut loose from every restraint. Sara was so perceptive. Didn't she guess the effect she had on him?

Sara looked at him and her heart gave a mighty leap. Jason was looking at her in a way that said his mind wasn't on any vitamins.

He'd stopped working on her calf and was rubbing his hand up and down her leg. He reached the sensitive area at the back of her knee and rested his hand there.

"Sara, I want to take you back to bed with me." Jason wanted to remove the blue dress that had driven him crazy all evening, undo her hair and run his hands through it till it flowed in a silky curtain over her bare shoulders. He wanted to watch her face as she removed his shirt, haul her close till bare skin rested against bare skin, and kiss her senseless.

Maybe she was allergic to the salmon fish cakes with sorrel sauce that she'd had for dinner. Maybe the reaction was affecting her hearing and her willpower.

"Wh-what did you say?"

"I want to make love with you, Sara."

She waited, but nothing else came; no declaration of love, of even liking. As direct as always, Jason had simply stated what was on his mind.

He waited. He hadn't put his heart on the line this way for the longest time, but he couldn't hold his love back any longer. To hell with being noble.

"Sara?"

She wet her lips. "I c-can't. I'm sorry, Jason."

He let go off her leg, putting a hand on her arm.

"Why not, Sara?"

Because unless he loved her back, making love with Jason would destroy her. Her mother had told her that memories of Cole Adams's love had sustained her all her life. More than anything, Sara wanted to lie in Jason's arms, to explore the realm of love with him. Only Jason hadn't used the word love.

She said the first thing that came into her mind. "I don't want to get involved right now, Jason. It would only complicate everything."

She was right. He stood and turned away. The fact she liked kissing him didn't mean she wanted to marry him. Involvement would interfere with Sara's dreams of freedom.

"You're right. I wasn't thinking straight." Jason ran a hand over his face. He'd better take another cold shower and try to get some sleep.

Jason filled his week with work and meetings for the next three days. When he couldn't stand it a minute longer, he decided to go home early.

Sara didn't have to be told he was avoiding her; she stayed out of his way. It was a surprise when she heard his key turn in the lock at three o'clock one afternoon.

Her breath caught in her throat at the sight of him in the kitchen doorway. "One of the Bintys' daughters fell and broke her ankle," she said quickly. "I gave them two days off."

Jason frowned. "You'll have to manage Kelsey on your own. I have a dinner meeting tonight."

"That's no problem."

"That's fine then." He nodded and left the room.

Sara took a deep breath. That had been rough but not as difficult as she'd anticipated. Jason had acted as if nothing had changed, and she would take her cue from him. She'd forgotten to tell him Dee-dee had called from New York. She was visiting a cousin there. All was well in that quarter. In every quarter, Sara tried to convince herself.

The freedom she'd always wanted was just around the corner. There was no reason to feel as if a rug had just been pulled out from under her feet.

As she lay in bed later that night, Sara admitted the truth. Living on her own had lost its appeal. Next to being a part of Kelsey's life, of loving Jason, it seemed empty and lonely. Turning over on her stomach, Sara punched her pillow. Positive thinking no longer worked for her. She would just have to find a way to fill her empty future.

* * *

It had been stupid to think Sara would run into his arms, tell him she loved him. Driving back from his dinner engagement, Jason told himself to stop being a fool.

A line from the fairy tales she read Kelsey brought a wry smile to his lips. The prince had told his woman that he loved her and she'd fallen in love with him instantly. It wouldn't be like that for Sara and him. This particular Sleeping Beauty didn't see him as a prince.

Sara was in the kitchen fixing breakfast when Jason walked in the next morning.

"Good morning."

"Morning." Sara looked at him over her shoulder and then away. She was wearing one of her long skirts and a loose sweater. Her hair was pulled back the way she had worn it in the beginning.

Jason frowned. Was it another reminder that the playacting was over?

"Dee-dee called to say she'd arrived and settled in okay."

"Yes."

Guilt made an uncomfortable bodysuit. Kelsey smiled up at him and Jason bent to kiss her, noticing she had almost finished her scrambled eggs and bacon. "Want some more juice?" he asked.

Kelsey nodded and he poured some juice into her glass.

Sara transferred scrambled eggs from the pan onto his plate. "The Bintys called to say they'd be back tomorrow morning."

Sara placed his plate in front of him and turned to glance at Kelsey's.

"Mine," she said, swiping the last piece of bacon off the little girl's plate and putting it into her mouth. Kelsey dissolved into giggles.

Jason looked from Sara's smiling face to his daughter's laughing one. How was he going to explain Sara's departure to his daughter, fill the void left behind?

"What's wrong? Did I put too much salt in the eggs?"

Jason was staring at them as if they were raw.

"They're perfect. I was just thinking of something else." He picked up his fork and began to eat. "I have a dinner meeting and I won't be back till late. Peter will know where to reach me if you need me."

I'll always need you. Sara poured herself a cup of tea and wrapped both hands around the cup.

"What are your plans for today?"

Sara looked surprised. Jason usually left in a hurry in the mornings. "Kelsey and I will go to the park for an hour in the morning, and then after lunch and her nap, we'll watch the videotape of *101 Dalmatians.*"

Jason wanted to suggest taking a picnic into the country, but he thought better of it. It would be harder to control his feelings in a relaxed setting.

He wished Sara would say something, instead of watching him silently. Her eyes had sent him a dozen silent messages just the way they were doing now.

What did Sara want from him?

Sara wished Jason wouldn't look at her that way. There was a certain intensity in his eyes that flamed the fires in her stomach to a blaze. At this rate she was never going to get them under control. His gaze indicated he was waiting for her to say something, only she didn't know what to say.

What did Jason want from her?

"Well, I'd better be—"

"Kelsey, honey, are you ready—"

They both stopped. Jason picked up his jacket and said, "Both of you have a nice day."

"You, too." Sara started clearing the table, wishing she didn't feel quite so empty. It was a feeling she'd have to get used to.

"Want to read that new book Grandma bought?" she asked Kelsey as she heard the front door close. "We can get your plastic tunnel out after that."

Action, lots of it, was the only way to keep thoughts at bay.

It was her search for an envelope for her letter to Claire that took her to Jason's office later that day. Going around his desk, she bent to open the drawer when she caught sight of the picture.

Sara walked over to the king-size bed. It was an eight-by-ten framed photograph of her in the red dress. She knew it was here to convince Dee-dee that their engagement was real. Why had Jason put it on his nightstand instead of his desk?

Sara picked it up, recalling the photo session at Rudolfo's. Ramon, the photographer, had coaxed her into so many different poses.

Pretend you're looking at the man you love, and you see his love for you in his eyes, he'd said as he'd taken this one.

She'd thought of Jason. Her eyes were full of dreams in the picture. Dreams that would never come true now.

Picking up the picture, she carried it out of the study. There was no need for it here, now that Dee-dee had left.

Jason stared at the papers on his desk and then looked at the clock—3:00 p.m. It would take another half hour to finish what he was doing. Never had a day, or his work, dragged so badly.

Now that he'd arrived at a decision, he wanted to get back early, to spend some time with Sara and Kelsey. Once the Bintys got back, things would be different. He'd have to tell

Sara soon about Dee-dee's dropping the case…it wasn't fair to keep it from her.

It also wasn't fair to keep Sara from what she wanted most. He was glad he'd subdued the impulse to tell Sara they had to extend their stay in England by another month. The temptation to keep her with him, hoping she would fall in love with him if she had enough time, was very strong.

Jason took another look at the papers in front of him. Sitting here, staring at them, wasn't accomplishing anything. He'd do it at home later tonight. He looked around for a floppy disk to transfer his work to.

Sara was humming over something in the kitchen when she heard Jason's key turn in the lock. Her heart began to pound. She had wanted to shower and change before he got home. Kelsey wasn't up from her nap yet and Sara had decided to finish the Irish stew she was making.

"Hi!"

Jason paused in the doorway and Sara let her eyes linger on the way the white shirt he wore emphasized the breadth of his shoulders.

"Hello, Jason."

Three more freckles had popped out on her nose this morning, her hair was tied back with the shoelace Kelsey had found behind the couch this morning, and the dark blue cotton sweater she wore with the white and blue skirt did nothing for her.

Jason took a deep breath. Whatever Sara was making smelled really good. She looked beautiful with that smudge of flour on her nose. Her hair stuck in damp curls to her forehead, and he fought the urge to pick her up and carry her into the shower with him.

"You're home early. Kelsey's still asleep."

"I know she doesn't get up from her nap till five. I wanted to talk to you about something, Sara, if you have a minute?" Jason pulled out a chair, turned it and straddled it.

"Of course." Sara turned away to stir whatever it was she was making.

"I want you to come sit down and give me all your attention."

"Oh." She turned the flame lower. Coming to the table, she pulled a chair out and sat down.

"I think my work here will be over by next week. We could leave for the States on Friday."

Sara looked surprised. "So soon?"

They'd only been here four weeks, and he'd mentioned six originally.

Jason nodded. "I know you're eager to get on with your own life. I've called Rowena and told her to hire some extra help to assist the Bintys. I'll release you from your contract as soon as possible."

"I see." She'd always known it had to end sometime, yet nothing had prepared her for the pain. Counting the week in Rainbow Valley, she'd known him for five weeks. Did she have enough memories to sustain her through a lifetime of loneliness?

"Have you thought about what you'd like to do when we get back?"

"What's going to happen about Dee-dee and the case?"

"She doesn't have to know your plans right away. We'll think of something to tell her later."

She was too hurt to ask Jason where all his determination to win the case had gone. Maybe he'd also sensed the subtle change in Dee-dee that she had noticed.

"In that case, I'll look for an apartment and find another job." The original dream had lost all its lure.

"It isn't going to be easy. California still hasn't pulled out of the recession yet."

"Something will turn up."

"Sara, do you think the terms of the contract were fair on you?"

"Of course."

"I don't think the money I'm paying you is enough for all you've done for us, Sara. I want to give you some more."

"You've done more than enough for me."

He frowned. "Living on your own can be very expensive. You'll need a car, too. It isn't going to be easy till you find another job."

He was worrying over her as if she were Kelsey's age. "I'm an adult, Jason, and adults face these situations all the time."

"Rowena said there was an opening in our office...."

More charity? "No, thank you, Jason. I want to make a fresh start all on my own."

"Sara, I respect your wish to do just that, but I can never repay what you've done for Kelsey. If you need any money, or anything at all, I want you to know I'll always be there for you."

It all boiled down to gratitude. Nothing more. "Thank you, Jason. If you'll excuse me, I've got a few more things to finish up in here."

Jason stood under the shower a few minutes later, telling himself he was a fool. Would he never learn? Sara didn't love him, or she would never have discussed leaving so coolly. He must have imagined the flicker of hurt in her eyes he'd first seen.

They were both quiet at the dinner table, preoccupied with their own thoughts.

Jason looked at Sara as she bustled between stove and kitchen table getting things, and frowned. He should have mentioned earlier that he'd asked Moses to put double the amount they'd originally agreed on into her account at the bank.

The silence made her uneasy, so Sara decided to talk to Kelsey. "I've sliced a cucumber for you. You like cucumbers, don't you? And after that we're having Irish stew and home-baked bread."

Sara placed a few slices of cucumber on Kelsey's plate and then her own, before passing the dish to Jason. The easiest way to get Kelsey to eat her vegetables was to serve them alone, first.

Jason hadn't said a word to her since she'd sent Kelsey into his room to bring him in to dinner.

"I forgot. Mrs. Binty made some special dressing for the cucumbers. You might like some."

She stood to get it out of the refrigerator and was just turning when she saw Kelsey reach out to her plate and pick up the last slice of cucumber from it. Grinning up at Sara, she said "Mine" loudly and clearly before she bit into it.

Jason looked up as if he'd been shot. Sara stared at Kelsey, her heart giving a great big leap.

"What's that?" Sara heard Jason ask hoarsely.

"Mine," Kelsey repeated with a giggle, putting the rest of the cucumber into her mouth.

"Jason, she spoke." Sara set the bowl of dressing on the table with a thud and clutched at Jason's arm. "Kelsey spoke."

He rose from the table, reaching for his daughter, and hugged her hard. "Oh, baby!" he said, his voice choked with tears.

Sara went up to them and put her arms around both of them. Tears streamed down her face as Jason lifted his face and she saw the reflection of her own tears in his eyes.

Kelsey wiggled in his arms, impatient to get back to her dinner. Jason put her back in her chair and reached for Sara. "Thank you for always believing she would."

They had no adult audience, but Jason put everything he had into the kiss. It started off soft and gentle, but then suddenly his mouth was making a different kind of demand, a demand that made Sara's legs tremble, made her want something she couldn't quite define.

Jason lifted his head and Sara realized her arms were around his neck. Not only that, but she seemed to be tugging him toward her again. Sara dropped her hands. What on earth was wrong with her? Jason was just sharing his happiness, but she was making a fool of herself. Sara sat down, her legs shaky. Kelsey, the least concerned of the three, had reached for the bowl of dressing, poured it all over her plate and was eating it with a spoon.

"Eat," she admonished the two grown-ups when they stared at her.

Sara and Jason exchanged a look and burst out laughing. Later that night Sara thanked the patron saint of children for helping matters along.

Sara hadn't thought about it when Kelsey had said her first word, but she did two days later at the breakfast table with Kelsey; Jason had his happy-ever-after ending. With Kelsey saying one more new word each day, the little girl would soon be talking nonstop. So much for her last hope that he might ask her to stay on for Kelsey's sake.

Sara tried to picture herself in an apartment near Claire, with a nine-to-five job and time to write and send out her short stories. She would even have time to join a local writers' group. The pictures didn't have the golden glow they once did. Instead the future seemed awash with the bitumen gray of loneliness.

Jason came into the kitchen. A quick look at Sara's face and he turned away to pour himself a cup of coffee. Staring out the kitchen window, she hadn't noticed him.

"Dada!" Kelsey banged on the table with her spoon and held her hands out for attention. It was the first time she'd said the word and it electrified Sara. She glanced over her shoulder to see Jason by the counter. His face was a study of emotions and her throat closed up.

He came over, picked Kelsey up and hugged her. The little girl patted his head and said on a note of discovery, "Dada!"

She wanted Jason to have a little time alone with Kelsey. After all, this was the moment every father waited for. Jason placed a hand on her shoulder and stopped her as she passed him, though he addressed his daughter. "Well, you finally decided to say Dada, did you, punkin? I'm glad there are only three words ahead of Dada— 'mine,' 'eat' and 'no-no.' For a minute there I thought I was going to come after shoes and potty. Now, how about saying Sara? C'mon, you can do it."

But Kelsey had lost interest in expanding her vocabulary. Mrs. Binty entered the kitchen and the three-year-old held her arms out to her. She was ready to go to the park.

Mrs. Binty took her from Jason and put her back in her chair. "Yes, we'll go feed the duckies, but you've got to eat your porridge first, darlin'. You need your strength to walk in the park."

Over Kelsey's head, Sara looked at Jason. He couldn't take his eyes off his daughter's face, and she was glad for his sake. Dee-dee didn't have an argument for her case now. Sara's hardest challenge lay ahead. She had to let go of all this with as much grace and dignity as she could muster.

Chapter Ten

At the last minute something came up that changed Jason's plans to return to the States with them. A phone call from Rome opened up the possibilities of a new business deal. A representative was flying out to talk to him about it, but it meant staying on for a day or more.

"It wouldn't make sense to change all our plans," he told Sara. "Why don't you, Kelsey, and the Bintys go on ahead, and I'll be there Sunday or Monday?"

"That's no problem."

Jason frowned. Sara seemed very quiet. He'd thought she'd be happy about returning to the States.

"Did you call the editor?"

"Yes." She'd finally picked up enough courage to do so, telling herself that she needed something to look forward to. "He wants to publish the article in the next issue of his magazine, and is interested in any more articles I might have."

"That's great. You must be looking forward to being able to give more time to your writing. Rowena's lined up some-one to help in the house, so Mrs. Binty can devote all her time to Kelsey. We'll try to arrange it so you can leave as quickly as possible."

Sara didn't say anything, though words welled up in her like the rising tide.

Jason looked at Sara. Was she feeling bad about leaving Kelsey? He knew how much Sara cared for Kelsey, how much she worried about her.

"You're welcome to visit Kelsey whenever you feel like it."

"Thank you."

He couldn't have made things clearer. She was already on the outside. A *visitor*, not a member of the household. "I'll start looking for an apartment as soon as I get back. Claire said her building might have a vacancy."

They'd driven Claire back one night when her car had re-fused to start. Jason hadn't liked the area she lived in. He didn't like the thought of Sara living there. He wanted to tell her that she could stay with them, that he would see she got all the freedom she wanted. Controlling the impulse, Jason folded the paper he'd opened and rose. Putting her in a cage, however large and pretty, would be denying Sara what she wanted most.

He paused by the door. "You have a good day."

"You, too."

Sara stared at her oatmeal after Jason left. The look of the hot cereal matched the future exactly. Dull, boring, *in-sipid*.

"Have a g'day. Have a g'day," Kelsey said over and over.

Sara reached over and used her napkin to wipe the little girl's mouth. "That's clever, Kelsey," she said with a catch in her voice, realizing she wouldn't be around too much longer to watch all the changes in the little girl. Maybe Mrs. Binty would give her daily accounts over the phone.

"Something's wrong, I tell you," Mrs. Binty said to her husband over their own breakfast. "Himself's working like the devil's after him, and our Sara's looking as if the bottom's dropped out of her world."

"Now, Mother. He's just busy with work and maybe she's a little sad about going back. We might leave them to arrange their own lives."

"Phooey," his wife said. "You heard Sara say more than once we're family. We've got a right to be interested in them. She's the only one I've worked for who hasn't treated us like servants. I care about her and I want her to be happy."

"So do I, but they may have changed their minds about getting married."

"If they break their engagement, I'm leaving. I'll go live with Sara and take care of her, that I will, and I'm going to give Himself a piece of my mind before I do that. I thought he was slow, not daft. He'll never find someone like our Sara. Never."

"Let's not cross our bridges before we come to them."

Sara couldn't understand why she felt so restless. They had been back in Rainbow Valley four days. Jason had been here for two, but she hadn't seen him yet. She heard Kelsey talking and laughing with him before he left in the morning, but she'd stayed in her room till she heard his car leave.

On the domestic front, things were going well. The new maid, Carmenita Sanchez, a young married woman, got on well with the Bintys and Kelsey. Dee-dee called every day to talk to a delighted Kelsey. Listening to the three-year-old talk nineteen words to the dozen filled everyone's heart with joy.

Sara had made her own plans. Claire's building did have a vacancy and she'd put a deposit on her apartment. She'd

tell Jason today that she was moving out tomorrow...
there was no point in staying on now.

She'd called her editor again and he'd mentioned the
magazine might offer her a permanent column. Encouraged by her writing success, but knowing it would be quite
a while before she could support herself with it, Sara had
filled out an application at an employment agency, stating
she would like a job where her writing skills could be used.

She was working on a puzzle with Kelsey when the phone
rang Wednesday evening. To her surprise, it was a call from
Margo Evans, the owner of the employment agency. An
advertising firm in Sherman Oaks had an opening. Was she
interested?

Sara did some quick thinking. Sherman Oaks was sev-
enty-five miles from Rainbow Valley. If she moved there to
be close to work, it would be hard to see Kelsey as often as
she wanted to.

"That's too far away. I want to stay in the area."

Margo said she'd keep looking, and hung up.

Sara stared into space. What if that was the only job she
could get? What if her money ran out and she hadn't found
another one?

"What's too far away?"

Sara spun around and her heart constricted. Jason looked
thinner, more tired. Mrs. Binty had mentioned that he came
in late and left early. He was working much too hard.

"Hello, Jason." Her heart pounded, her mouth went dry,
and her breath was stuck somewhere in the middle of her
chest.

"How are you, Sara? What's too far away?" He repeated, picking up his daughter and kissing her. Kelsey
wiggled to be put down, her attention on the puzzle she was
working on.

"A job in Sherman Oaks."

"Far away from what?"

From you, you blind fool, Sara wanted to yell, angry with herself for reacting like this to his presence, angry that she couldn't control the way she felt.

She wet her lips. "I want to be close enough to see Kelsey once in a while."

There. She'd managed to keep her voice nice and light, as if it was just a friendly interest she had in his daughter.

He frowned. "Jobs aren't easy to find, Sara."

It hurt that he should keep pushing that point. Did he think he was stuck with her till she did find one? He'd turned away, as if about to leave, when she said, "I've found a place to stay. I'm moving out tomorrow."

He stopped and turned toward her. Sara moved a step back.

The only reason she could think of for the anger in his eyes was her rejection of his lovemaking. In spite of all the hurt, Sara was glad she had. She wasn't beautiful, or rich, or even very clever, but she did know she couldn't give herself to a man who didn't love her. Not even to Jason.

A tight look had come over his face as he'd scanned her features, then he said, "Do you need help moving?"

"No, thank you, Jason. Claire and I can manage between us." She wasn't going to tell him she wasn't taking any of the fancy clothes he'd bought her. They belonged to this time of her life...a period she had to seal away and try to forget.

Jason's eyes rested on his daughter's head. He thought of the day he'd gone to pick Sara up. She'd stood in her uncle's house, holding her cardboard box tied with string and he'd wondered if he was doing the right thing hiring her. Now he didn't know what he would do without her.

"I've told Kelsey I have to go away," Sara said softly. "Mrs. Binty's been doing everything for her since we got back from London, so the transition won't upset Kelsey's routine. I'll call her every day in the beginning, then gradually taper it off.''

''Thank you, Sara.'' A slow burn had started in his chest at the deep sadness in Sara's voice. It made his voice harsher than he intended. ''I'll have your last check ready for you Friday.''

Something inside Sara shriveled as Jason looked at her as if she were a stranger. All she could say was, ''Thank you.''

Jason carried the memory of her face around all evening. Dammit, she was getting exactly what she wanted, so why had she looked hurt when he'd mentioned having her check ready? He didn't understand her. She needed the security of a job and yet she turned down the chance of getting one saying she wanted to be near Kelsey.

Did she think he was blind? That he couldn't see how much she loved Kelsey? Sara didn't hold back when she made a commitment, and a part of him was glad she'd made one to Kelsey. His daughter's life would be richer for having someone like Sara in it. His own pain he'd have to learn to handle.

He was so distracted all evening that the business acquaintance he was having dinner with asked him if something was wrong. Jason told Jake Ramsey that he wasn't feeling well.

It wasn't a lie. The emptiness inside was growing with each hour that passed at the thought that Sara would soon be gone. He wondered how the little gosling that had gone to London had taken the news of Sara's departure. Knowing Sara, preparing Kelsey for it wasn't a responsibility she would have shirked.

''Why don't we get together sometime next week when you're feeling better?''

The thought of Sara on her own, having to find work, struggling to make ends meet, bothered him.

"Jason?" The touch on his arm startled him. He looked at Jake Ramsey's concerned face.

"I'm sorry." He rubbed his forehead. "What were you saying?"

"I said, let's get together next week when you're feeling better. In the meantime, take care of whatever it is you have."

Whatever it was he had.

As he drove home, Jason realized this was the one thing he couldn't take care of. There was no antilock braking device for love that he could invent.

For a moment he felt very strongly that he had to go home and tell Sara how he felt. His foot pressed the accelerator to the floor. Maybe she would still be up.

He was a desperate man, standing on the lip of a dark and lonely chasm that he would fall into when Sara left. He had to try to keep her with him. When Diana had died, all he'd felt was pity for her and regret that they hadn't had a better life together.

The thought of Di shocked Jason into facing reality. What would happen if he persuaded Sara to marry him? Maybe she wouldn't mind being his wife, being Kelsey's mother for a while, but later, when she found his daughter's demands too great, or she got pregnant...what would happen then?

Jason's hands tightened on the wheel as he thought of Diana's face, contorted with anger, telling him he had tricked her into getting pregnant, just so he could tie her down.

He could never run the risk of that happening with Sara. He had to let her go, take his chances and wait. He would make sure he saw her often, remind her that he was around.

Taking his foot off the accelerator, Jason checked the sideview mirror and changed lanes. He would take the long way home. Driving around would give him time to calm down.

Sara woke at five Thursday morning. Tomorrow would make six weeks since she'd first met Jason. She was glad now that she'd moved in here right away, that she had more time to spend with him and Kelsey. She wished they could have stayed in London longer, been together for a little more time, but that couldn't be.

It was no use trying to go back to sleep. Thoughts of Jason had kept her awake till she'd heard his car pull into the garage at one this morning.

Sara looked around. The single suitcase she'd bought was already packed, so there was nothing to do. She didn't want to work on her writing. The only thing that might help her calm down was physical work. She decided to take her whole room apart, take all the books down and wipe the shelves and dust them, so Carmenita would have one less thing to do after she left.

Fetching some rags from the kitchen, Sara looked through the window. Her heart jumped into her throat. Jason was on the deck in the back, staring at the mountains, a mug of coffee in his hand. Her eyes widened as she took in the dress pants and the white silk shirt he'd worn to his dinner meeting. Hadn't he gone to bed at all?

That must have been some meeting. The thought that he might have been with a woman aroused such a storm of jealousy in Sara that she wanted to march out there and confront him. But she didn't. Jason had made it very clear it wasn't her he wanted, anyway, and his personal life wasn't any of her business.

As Sara removed the books and wiped the shelves down with furniture polish, she tried to figure out why life was so strange. Why had Jason just wanted her, not loved her? Was it because in spite of the fact that he'd bought her expensive clothes and tried to introduce her to his kind of life, she had failed in some way?

Sara swept the books off the next shelf. She couldn't be anything else than what she was...ordinary, plain, homely. As she picked up another pile of books, Sara realized Kelsey had carried one of Jason's automotive magazines in and left it in the room. It slipped off the top of the pile of books and slid down to the carpet. Sara picked it up and a sheet of paper slipped out.

The paper she held was too thin to be a picture. Turning it over, she scanned the first two lines.

She had to read the letter through twice before she could absorb the contents. From Dee-dee, the note informed Jason that, as per the talk they'd had, she'd told her attorney that she was dropping the case. She apologized for all the tension she had created and thanked him and Sara for giving her another chance with Kelsey.

Sara's gaze flew to the date. Jason must have received this in London. And all this time she'd hoped and prayed that Dee-dee would drop the case.

What kind of a man would keep a letter like this from her?

So mad she could hardly breathe, Sara marched out of the room. Jason Graham had some explaining to do.

He was still out on the deck. Sara flung open the patio door and launched into her attack right away.

"Why didn't you tell me about this?"

He swung around at the sound of her voice and her anger went into an immediate nosedive. Unshaven, the top four buttons of his shirt undone, Jason looked exhausted.

"Tell you about what?" he asked wearily.

She held the letter out, telling herself she was still very angry. "It's from Dee-dee. You must have gotten it in London."

"Yes."

"Why didn't you tell me?"

"I'm sorry." He turned away as if the view was the most important thing around. His wooden tone made her look at his back in exasperation. He didn't add anything and she stared at the letter in frustration.

Suddenly she knew what kind of a man would keep the letter a secret. The only possibility pushed the dark clouds of anger aside. A joy so heady it made her pulses race began to seep through her system. Sara breathed a prayer for help to the patron saint of love.

"I'm going to sue you, Jason," she said as seriously as she could manage.

"What?" He swung around and looked at her.

"I'm going to sue you," Sara repeated, hoping her courage wouldn't fail before she got through with this.

"What for?"

"Breach of promise."

"Breach of promise?"

"You said we had to be honest with each other. By hiding the letter, you broke our contract."

The look in Sara's eyes gave Jason his first clue that something else was afoot. There was a new light in them that had nothing to do with anger. Cautiously he asked, "What are you going to sue me for?"

He would gladly give her everything he had.

"I'm going to take you for all you've got—your heart, your body, Kelsey, and shares in the rest of your life."

He felt as if he'd been punched in the stomach. Sara wanted it all? He had to tell her how he felt. "I hid the letter because I wanted you to stay longer."

"I beg your pardon?"

"I said, I wanted you to stay, dammit. I hoped that if you stayed a little longer that you might begin to like us too much to leave."

"Don't swear, Jason. I've more than liked you for a very long time," she confessed. "You're the one who insisted I leave."

"That's because just liking isn't enough. Nor is staying because you love Kelsey. I want—" He broke off abruptly, then said, "Oh hell, what's the use? You need to experience freedom, Sara. You need to try your wings, so that you won't blame me for clipping them later."

"What do *you* want Jason?" she asked, her heart pounding at his words.

"I want your love, Sara. I want to spend the rest of my life with you, but I won't take your dream of freedom away."

Hope began to play the opening bars of a symphony of happiness. "My dream isn't cast in stone, Jason. I've realized I don't have to be on my own to experience freedom. Can't I experience it right here with you? Isn't freedom simply protecting the basic right to choose what you do?"

"Certain situations can deprive you of that freedom, Sara."

"What kind of situations?"

"Marriage, a child, getting pregnant."

The opening bars moved into a crescendo of love. "Is this a firm offer?"

"Sara—" Jason reached for her shoulders, unable to stop himself "—don't tempt me."

Sara smiled at him, tenderness sweeping through her at the look in his eyes. "Jason, I want to tempt you right out of your mind. That's what you've done to me. You've taken over my head, my heart, my whole life. I know I'll never stop being free with you. I love you."

His grip on her shoulders tightened as he searched her face for the truth. "Love doesn't last forever, Sara. The fires die down and the ashes grow cold."

"I know people don't always burn at the same rate as they do in the beginning when their love is new, but the fire doesn't go out for everybody. Look at Peter and Meera. As long as we're willing to tend the flames and work at keeping them burning, they won't die down."

"That's easy to say now. You'll hate me when reality begins to creep in. You'll blame me for taking away your chances. Dashed hopes will douse any fire."

"Realistic hopes don't have to be dashed, Jason. I know what I want. I want you, and Kelsey, and any other children we may have together. I also want to write. But what do you want out of life?"

"You. Kelsey. To make Graham Electronics the best business of its kind."

"None of those are unrealistic dreams, Jason."

She was right.

Sara had had enough of talking for the time being. She put her arms around Jason and kissed him three times. "That's yes, yes and yes."

"Yes, yes and yes to what?" He lifted a brow, though his eyes glowed with love as his arms went around her and hauled her close.

"Yes to marrying you, yes to loving Kelsey, yes to getting pregnant."

"What about your writing?"

"I don't think I'll ever stop writing. Loving you, having a family, is going to make my writing richer not poorer."

Jason picked Sara up and spun her around.

"I'm going to draw up another agreement," he said when he set her down.

"And the terms?"

"The terms are unconditional and unlimited love for the rest of our lives, and as much care, time and attention as it will take to make sure this fire never dies down."

He kissed her till they were both breathless, and then he said, "I'm taking on a junior partner, Jake Ramsey, who's going to take care of all the marketing. That'll free me up to concentrate on research at the plant, and you and Kelsey won't have to move around so much. We can convert one of the bedrooms into a study for you, or would you rather rent office space?"

"I want to write right here," Sara said, her eyes on the mountains. "I don't want to miss any of Kelsey's growing up. Besides, there's another bonus to working at home."

"Which is?" Jason lifted her hand and pressed his lips to the back of her fingers.

Sara's smile widened into a grin. "When the boss comes home for two-hour lunches, I'll be right here."

"Sara, I don't think I have ever been so scared of losing you as I was in the last week." Jason kissed her as if he would never let her go. "And now I can't believe you're really going to marry me."

"I can't believe it, either."

From the kitchen, the Bintys looked on approvingly.

"Now there's a nice turn of events," Mrs. Binty said to her husband. "Makes a body feel good."

She turned away. "Will you listen for the little one waking? I have to make a phone call from our bedroom."

"At this hour?"

"It's to Mrs. Smythe. She lost her bet and she owes me a hundred pounds."

"A hundred pounds?" Mr. Binty looked horrified. "That's almost one hundred and fifty American dollars! How could you place a bet with Himself's mother-in-law?"

"She said they wouldn't wrap it up so quickly, that Sara would move out before Himself realized what he'd lost and go after her. I said she wouldn't move out at all...he wouldn't let her. I won."

"It's not right," Mr. Binty protested.

"Oh, hush your grumbling. You wanted this as much as I did. Why shouldn't I bet on something I'm sure of? Look at them and tell me love doesn't win when it's strong and true."

Mr. Binty turned to look at the couple outside the window. Locked in each other's embrace, they looked like they needed some privacy. He turned away and hurried after his wife just in time to hear her say, "There's always a happily ever-after for those who believe in it. Always."

Epilogue

"Sara!"

She turned her head and smiled at the sound of Jason's voice. He'd come home early.

"I'm in here," she called.

He came into the nursery and smiled. "How are you doing?"

"I'm fine, Jason." She smiled down at her son, who nursed at her breast as if he was starving.

"And Justin?" He came nearer and touched the top of his son's head very tenderly.

"He's busy, as you can see."

Their gazes met over Justin's dusty blond head, and the intensity she recognized now crept into Jason's eyes.

"I love you, Sara." He leaned forward and kissed her lightly. "You're so beautiful."

Sara smiled through the tears that gathered in her eyes. "I love you, too, Jason. Thank you for filling my life with love and happiness."

Love had filled her life with all the colors of the rain
bow; the deep lavender of absolute contentment, the tru
blue of a lasting love, the vibrant green of family.

"Are you feeling all right?" Jason asked anxiously. "Yc
look pale. Should I call Dr. Rushmore?"

"Jason, of course I'm looking pale. It's only four da;
since Justin was born. As for calling Dr. Rushmore, did yc
call the poor woman and ask if you could have a separa
line put into her office? Give the poor woman a break."

"I will if you're sure you're all right."

Sara lifted a hand and touched his face. "Stop worryin
I'm fine. Mrs. Binty's hardly left my side all day. Kelsey sa
she wanted to stay home and take care of us, too, but
managed to persuade her to go to preschool. All I do is e
and rest and feed Justin. Isn't he beautiful?"

Jason touched his son's hand with a finger, delight
when the tiny fingers closed over his. He still hadn't reco
ered from seeing Justin slip out of Sara's body, a warr
wailing scrap of humanity, testimony of their love for ea
other. "He's beautiful, Sara."

"Daddy, can I come in now?"

Jason swung around to the door. "Of course, honey."

Kelsey rushed in. "Mama, there's a surprise for you her
and Daddy said I could bring it to you."

"Thanks, Kelsey." She'd adopted Kelsey legally soon a
ter she and Jason were married, thrilled when Kelsey ha
started calling her Mama.

"First I have to give you three messages." Kelsey held
three fingers. "Aunty Meera called and asked when we we
going to London. She wants to see me 'n' Justin. Clai
called and asked if I've taught Justin to say damn yet, li
Daddy does." She stared at the third finger she'd held up f
a while before her face brightened. "Oh, yes, Binty said
tell you Grandma called when you were sleeping and want
to know if she could come over tonight."

Jason looked surprised. "She's been here every night."

Sara nodded. Dee-dee couldn't have been more excited about Justin's birth if he'd been her own grandson. Sara was grateful that the past year had seen Jason and Dee-dee developing a more friendly relationship. "She's a wonderful grandmother. If only she wouldn't keep buying so many presents."

They looked around Justin's room, and then at each other and smiled. It was chock-full with oversize stuffed toys. Some things never changed.

"Is Justin hungry again?" Kelsey demanded.

The disgust in her voice made her parents smile.

"Babies have very small stomachs, and so they get hungry often," Sara explained to the four-year-old. "Why don't you unwrap the package for me?"

Kelsey ripped the paper off. Sara's breath caught in her throat at the sight of the beautiful leather-bound book Kelsey held out to her.

Her name was embossed in large gold letters on the burgundy background: *Essays by Sara Graham.*

Sara couldn't believe what Jason had done for her. All the essays she had written for the magazine were reprinted inside on fine vellum bond.

"Oh, Jason. When did you have this done?"

"I ordered it a month ago."

"Thank you." Tears filled Sara's eyes. Jason was always so proud of her work.

He had slipped a piece of paper into the book. Sara pulled it out. *In commemoration of the birth of our son, Justin Cole Graham,* the words on the paper said.

"Oh, Jason," Sara said again, close to tears.

Tired of the way her parents kept looking at each other, Kelsey said something about calling Grandma, and skipped out of the room. Sara put a hand on Jason's shoulder and leaned forward so she could kiss him. "I love you so much."

Mrs. Binty bustled in, took Justin from Sara and patted his back to burp him.

"Everything's ready, sir," she said to Jason.

"What's ready?" Sara asked, dragging her gaze away from the book.

Jason simply picked her up in his arms and carried her in the direction of the master suite. He stopped in the doorway, and Sara stared.

In front of the fireplace was a small table covered with a lace tablecloth. A log crackled in the fireplace and two candles had been lit on the table.

"Jason, what's all this?"

"A celebration, Sara. Remember what you once said about making sure those fires never go out? This is my contribution."

Sara touched her husband's face, in no hurry to be put down. "You make so many contributions, Jason. You love us all, you're a good husband and father. The Bintys mentioned today that they would stay on longer than the ten years they'd originally signed on for. 'Seeing as how we were going to keep them busy by having more babes' is how Mr. Binty put it."

Jason didn't know how Sara could talk of having another child so soon. He hadn't forgotten the discomfort and pain she'd endured to have Justin.

"Sara, I don't want any more children. I think two are more than enough."

"We're going to have two more children, Jason, but not right away, so don't start worrying about it," his wife said firmly. "Now, put me down. I'm starving."

Jason kissed her before he put her into her chair. Sitting down, he looked at the covered dishes Mrs. Binty had placed on the table. He was sure there was a good meal under them just as he was sure that Sara loved him, Kelsey and their newborn son.

He looked at Sara's glowing face and then bowed his head briefly to give thanks for his family and a love that would endure for a lifetime.

* * * * *

Get Ready to be Swept Away by
Silhouette's Spring Collection

Abduction & Seduction

These passion-filled stories explore both the dangerous
desires of men and the seductive powers of women.
Written by three of our most celebrated authors, they are
sure to capture your hearts.

Diana Palmer
Brings us a spin-off of her Long, Tall Texans series

Joan Johnston
Crafts a beguiling Western romance

Rebecca Brandewyne
New York Times bestselling author
makes a smashing contemporary debut

Available in March at your favorite retail outlet.

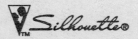

MILLION DOLLAR SWEEPSTAKES (III)

No purchase necessary. To enter, follow the directions published. Method of entry may vary. For eligibility, entries must be received no later than March 31, 1996. No liability is assumed for printing errors, lost, late or misdirected entries. Odds of winning are determined by the number of eligible entries distributed and received. Prizewinners will be determined no later than June 30, 1996.

Sweepstakes open to residents of the U.S. (except Puerto Rico), Canada, Europe and Taiwan who are 18 years of age or older. All applicable laws and regulations apply. Sweepstakes offer void wherever prohibited by law. Values of all prizes are in U.S. currency. This sweepstakes is presented by Torstar Corp., its subsidiaries and affiliates, in conjunction with book, merchandise and/or product offerings. For a copy of the Official Rules send a self-addressed, stamped envelope (WA residents need not affix return postage) to: MILLION DOLLAR SWEEPSTAKES (III) Rules, P.O. Box 4573, Blair, NE 68009, USA.

EXTRA BONUS PRIZE DRAWING

No purchase necessary. The Extra Bonus Prize will be awarded in a random drawing to be conducted no later than 5/30/96 from among all entries received. To qualify, entries must be received by 3/31/96 and comply with published directions. Drawing open to residents of the U.S. (except Puerto Rico), Canada, Europe and Taiwan who are 18 years of age or older. All applicable laws and regulations apply; offer void wherever prohibited by law. Odds of winning are dependent upon number of eligibile entries received. Prize is valued in U.S. currency. The offer is presented by Torstar Corp., its subsidiaries and affiliates in conjunction with book, merchandise and/or product offering. For a copy of the Official Rules governing this sweepstakes, send a self-addressed, stamped envelope (WA residents need not affix return postage) to: Extra Bonus Prize Drawing Rules, P.O. Box 4590, Blair, NE 68009, USA.

HE'S MORE THAN A MAN, HE'S ONE OF OUR

NANNY AND THE PROFESSOR
Donna Clayton

His son's new nanny taught Joshua Kingston a few things about child rearing. Now Joshua wanted to teach Cassie Simmons a few things about love. But could he persuade the elusive Cassie to be his wife?

Look for *Nanny and the Professor* by Donna Clayton, available in March.

Fall in love with our Fabulous Fathers!

Silhouette
R O M A N C E™

SAME TIME, NEXT YEAR
Debbie Macomber
(SE #937, February)

Midnight, New Year's Eve...a magical night with
Summer Lawton that James Wilken knew could never
be enough. So he'd spontaneously asked her to meet
him again in exactly one year's time. Now that time
had come...and with it, a friendly reunion that was
quickly turning to love!

Don't miss
SAME TIME, NEXT YEAR,
by Debbie Macomber,
available in February!

She's friend, wife, mother—she's you! And beside
each Special Woman stands a wonderfully
special man. It's a celebration of our heroines—
and the men who become part of their lives.

Don't miss **THAT SPECIAL WOMAN!** each month—
from some of your special authors! Only from
Silhouette Special Edition!

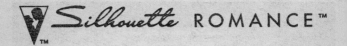

BELIEVING IN MIRACLES
by
Linda Varner

Carpenter Andy Fulbright and Honorine "Honey" Truman had all
the criteria for a perfect marriage—they liked and respected
each other, they desired and needed each other...and *neither*
one loved the other! But with the help of some mistletoe and
two young elves, these two might learn to believe in the miracle
of Christmas....

BELIEVING IN MIRACLES is the second book in Linda Varner's
MR. RIGHT, INC., a heartwarming series about three hardworking
bachelors in the building trade who find love at first sight—
construction site, that is!

Don't miss BELIEVING IN MIRACLES, available in December.
And look for Book 3, WIFE MOST UNLIKELY, in March 1995.
Read along as old friends make the difficult transition to
lovers....

Only from

where passion lives.